LOST AND FOUND

Tom Winter

corsair

Constable & Robinson Ltd
55–56 Russell Square
London WC1B 4HP
www.constablerobinson.com

First published in the UK by Corsair,
an imprint of Constable & Robinson, 2013

A copy of the British Library Cataloguing in Publication
Data is available from the British Library

ISBN 978-1-47210-159-4 (hardback)
ISBN 978-1-47210-489-2 (ebook)

Printed and bound in the UK

1 3 5 7 9 10 8 6 4 2

MIX
Paper from
responsible sources
FSC® C018072

For Juliet

CAROL

1

Carol wants a disease. Nothing deadly, and nothing crippling. She doesn't aspire to disabled parking, for instance, despite its obvious advantages.

'It's true I haven't done much with my life,' she wants to tell people, 'but it's the . . . the leprosy.'

She imagines how they would nod sympathetically, albeit while backing away, and even she might feel better about looking at herself in the mirror each morning: a middle-aged woman who hasn't accomplished much because she can't, because she's been too busy peeling off dead skin and looking for missing body parts.

'Yes,' she'd say, as she arrives at work late yet again, 'I know I'm crap at this, but the good news is I've found a couple of my fingers.'

But, no, there is no disease, no excuse to hide behind. She has a husband who's a certifiable dickhead, but this isn't her disability *per se*. And her daughter – well, what can she say on that subject? In the months prior to giving birth, she read every book on child-rearing she could find. In retrospect, Sun Tzu's *Art of War* would have been a better choice, or perhaps a field study of rabid primates.

Naturally, this isn't how she'd expected to feel about motherhood, but watching her baby daughter morph into a teenager has been an alarming experience, like cresting the first hill of a rollercoaster just as she realized her seatbelt was broken.

Now seventeen, her daughter stands on the cusp of independence, the whole world at her feet. And Carol is on a bus home, staring at a window too wet with rain to offer a view of anything; an indeterminate cityscape, as fractured and abstract as her own life – the hint of a street sign, the edge of a shop front, but nothing complete, nothing she can look at and say, 'Ah, that's where I am.'

So, nearly twenty years of married life have come to this: 'I'm leaving.'

She savours the words for a moment, already regretting that she'll only get to say them once. Condensing so many years of frustration into two small words has given them a curious, almost nuclear power, as if they might slip from her mouth and accidentally level the whole of London.

She knows she'll tell her husband over dinner tonight, though she still isn't sure how she'll raise the subject. The only certainty is that she'll serve a nicer dessert than usual – her favourite, as it happens – though she'll try her best to make this seem like an act of consolation rather than celebration.

2

IT'S STRIKING HOW much can change in twelve or thirteen miles. Carol has seen runners on half-marathons, everyone crossing the finishing line with rosy cheeks and broad smiles. The same cannot be said of London. In the twelve miles between Westminster and Croydon, London is reduced from a city of parks and palaces to this, an unrecognizable commuter belt, a grey concrete mess. To say London ends at Croydon is only half true: stripped of hope and worn down, London really crawls into Croydon and dies.

Of course, this isn't something people are inclined to admit in Carol's part of Croydon, where the overworked middle classes still want to believe in the dream – waxing their cars on Sunday afternoons, decorating their window ledges with scented candles and porcelain figurines.

Carol tries not to think about her neighbour's habits as she walks home from the bus stop, tries not to care that the whole estate is a labyrinth of cul-de-sacs, more a communal

Petri dish than a place to live. Tonight she will be cutting her ties to this place. Soon she will float free.

'Carol!' Mandy Horton comes running from a nearby house, her every move a clatter of bangles and costume jewellery. 'Bob and Tony are playing darts tonight. They want us to meet them at the pub.'

'What?'

'Bob and Tony—'

'No, I mean Bob never mentioned anything about going to the pub tonight.'

'So?' replies Mandy, with a dismissive snort.

For a brief moment, Carol wonders what those snorts would sound like if she held Mandy's head underwater, perhaps even kept it there, submerged, until she went limp and cold to the touch.

She realizes Mandy is talking.

'. . . and it is Tuesday. It's not like there's anything else to do.'

Carol steals a glance at her shopping bag, the dessert almost poking from the top. 'I was hoping to have a chat with Bob, that's all.'

'But you can do that at the pub, silly! How about I come by in thirty minutes?' Her eyes flit across Carol's dress, a hint of pity in her face. 'It'll give you time to change.'

When Carol gets home, the house has a burgled look: not messy so much as strewn, as if the entire building has been lifted from its foundations and kicked around while she was out.

She hesitates at the foot of the stairs, certain that her daughter Sophie is up there somewhere. For Carol, the fact that a teenager can achieve total invisibility in a modest three-bedroom home says it all: Sophie has guerrilla instincts that could put the Viet Cong and the Taliban to shame.

'Sophie?'

Silence.

She ponders going upstairs to say hello – perhaps have another stab at that mother-daughter thing she's aspired to for the last seventeen years – but then thinks better of it. The simple act of dialogue with Sophie has become so rare, it seems better to save the moment for when she has something important to say: 'Yes, I'm leaving', 'No, I'm not coming back'.

She feels a stab of guilt, not at the prospect of having that conversation, but at the possibility of enjoying it. It isn't that Sophie's a bad child, she's just not the sort Carol would have chosen had it been a mail-order process. The only things she really understands about her daughter are the qualities she inherited from Bob – an ability to reduce the house to chaos, for instance, and an expectation that Carol will always be there to deal with the aftermath. Everything else just seems oddly foreign and incomprehensible. Even her intelligence feels redolent of a manufacturing error: how could a bright, studious child have been assembled from this genetic material? It's a question Carol can't answer; a question that leaves her with the vague sense that, in getting the daughter everyone thinks they want, she missed out on the kind that could have loved and needed her.

Thinking the sound of the refrigerator being restocked might provoke a visceral reaction – after all, even clever people have to eat – she labours over the dessert: slowly peels away the packaging, carefully puts it on a plate, slides it into the refrigerator, with the heavy-handed clank of porcelain on metal.

In the loaded silence that follows, she decides she won't go to the pub tonight – might not even answer the door when Mandy arrives in the inevitable cloud of perfume. Instead, she'll wait for Bob to return and will then set about destroying their life together, much as a butterfly must destroy its cocoon in order to live.

3

Yes, she went to the pub after all, succumbing to the same emotional paralysis that has seen her spend years wanting to leave Bob but never quite finding the courage to make it happen; a life that has been dedicated to other people's happiness even at the expense of her own. Yet as she watches the evening unfold around her – a room full of people drinking to forget the futility of their own lives – she knows tonight is still the night she breaks free.

When the time finally comes for them to go home, Carol and Bob drive in an unusual silence, insulated from the tragedy of late-night Croydon by the suburban bubble of their three-door hatchback. Carol's heard of animals sensing earthquakes hours and even days beforehand. Is the same thing now happening with Bob? She glances at him behind the wheel, certain that if she could peel back his skull she'd find just a hollow, empty space, perhaps a single red light flashing in the darkness.

'I didn't expect it to be a pub night,' she says. It feels

good to initiate The Conversation, her first move towards freedom.

'No, it was a last-minute thing. I . . . I thought it'd be good to get out.'

'Actually, I was hoping we could talk.'

Bob looks alarmed. 'What – you and me?'

'Yes, Bob, you and me.'

His eyes widen, and for a moment Carol thinks he might be having some kind of aneurysm – a convenient end to her marriage, it's true, but not what she wants when travelling at sixty miles an hour.

'Bob, are you all right?'

Still those wide eyes.

'Bob? Bob, stop the car.'

Nothing.

'Bob! Pull over! Now!'

They begin to slow.

By the time they pull to a stop, Bob is slouched in his seat. 'You know, don't you?'

Carol stares at him, so confused she momentarily forgets that she's supposed to be leaving him. 'Know what?'

'That's why I wanted us to spend the night at the pub.'

'Bob—'

'You know, to relax.'

'Bob—'

'I thought it'd be a distraction.'

'For fuck's sake, just say it.'

He begins to cry. 'I've got a lump. On my testicle.'

'Oh, shit, I'm sorry . . .' She tries to reach for him, but

her seatbelt snags. She struggles to unbuckle it, turns to face him. 'Look, Bob, it's going to be all right.'

'I was hoping it would just go away, but . . .'

She holds his hands with an affection that surprises even her. 'Look, it's all okay. I understand.'

'I just thought a game of darts . . . I don't know, it sounds mad, but I thought it'd bring me luck.'

'And did you win?'

'No.' He begins crying harder.

'Bob . . .'

'What if I lose my balls?'

Even in the auto-pilot of Carol's compassion, it strikes her that Bob is a forty-something man in an almost sexless marriage – under the circumstances, his testicles became unnecessary baggage years ago.

'And what if it's spread?' he says, more panicked now.

'Bob, it might be nothing. Just a lump.'

He chokes back the tears. 'I don't want to die.'

And, right then, she does feel sorry for him, this grown man who's been reduced to helplessness.

'We're going to the doctor first thing in the morning, okay?'

She imagines the doctor laughing and telling them it's nothing, a mere physical expression of Bob's mental decrepitude. On their way home, Carol will tell him she doesn't love him, has never really loved him. With a sharp dose of reality and a course of antibiotics, both she and the lump will disappear from his life for ever.

And yet here he is, looking up at her, imploring,

desperate, terrified. 'God,' he says, 'I love you so much.'

'I know,' is all she can manage, but still he gazes at her, a frightened man with an ominous lump; a man for whom a few simple words would make all the difference.

'And I . . .' she adds, with barely a stammer '. . . I love you too.'

ALBERT

4

'I THINK IT's stuck.'

'Well, I know that, Albert.'

'Probably a loose stamp or something.'

Albert peers into the sorting machine with a fearful expression. It reminds him of the Hadron Collider he's seen on television, the one that's supposed to explain everything about the universe. The machine here at the Royal Mail sorting office is much smaller, of course – it doesn't loop beneath South London for forty miles or anything like that – but it still has a quality that makes Albert uneasy. He can remember the names of all the people it's replaced and, quite frankly, it's smarter than all of them put together, which only begs the question: why use something so clever just to sort envelopes into little piles? It's like asking Einstein to make a cup of tea.

'This thing has secrets,' he says, 'mark my words.'

'What's that, Albert?' The trainee screws up his face as he says it, evidently convinced that everything old people say is incomprehensible.

'I said I can't help you.'

'I didn't ask you to. The engineer's coming in an hour.'

That's something else that's changed, thinks Albert, as he trudges away. He can remember a time when the men nearing retirement were looked up to as heroes. A trainee would have felt privileged even to get a clip round the ear from one of them. Albert's not a man of imposing height or stature, it's true, but what remains of his hair is clearly grey, which should at least count for something.

'It's a world gone mad,' he mutters to himself. 'All the good men are dead and gone . . .'

Even though no one is listening, he regrets his choice of words. He's already scared of his impending retirement; he doesn't need to bring mortality into it too.

From across the room, a voice: 'You're a lucky bastard, Albert, you know that?'

He looks up to see his supervisor, Darren, approaching; a forty-something middle manager with a liking for clipboards.

'A few more weeks and it's all over for you, isn't it?' There's a moment of tense silence. 'The job, I mean. Get out of this place, the days free to do whatever you want.'

'I'd rather keep working.'

'Nah, you don't mean that.' He doesn't wait for a response. 'You know, I envy you, actually. Time for yourself, time to do some gardening—'

'I live in a flat.'

'Well, window boxes can be lovely. There's a real art to them too. And there's always the grandkids to keep you busy.'

Childless, Albert decides to let the comment pass. There's

something about having no family that always seems to alarm people. He can almost see the fear in their faces, that if he has no wife or children, maybe one day he might ask them to take him to the toilet or give him a bath.

'The theme parks are great for kids. I dare say they all offer discounts for pensioners.'

'If nothing else, my cat will be happy to have me around.' This is all Albert can say with conviction: that his cat, the only other living thing in his life, will continue to need and want him regardless.

'Well, there you go,' replies Darren. 'And kids love animals.' He looks at his watch in a practised, self-important way. 'You're the man of the moment, so let me know if there's anything you need, okay?'

He hurries away before Albert can reply – plead for his job, perhaps, or ask to be taken outside and shot.

Albert is still watching him go when one of the girls from the admin office approaches. 'Albert?' she says, with the awkward, wide-eyed look of someone delivering bad news. 'One of your neighbours just called. It's about your cat . . .'

5

At least Gloria isn't dead. She's awkward to carry in this position. And it's surprising how even a couple of legs in plaster make her so much heavier. But at least she isn't dead.

A younger cat might have handled the fall better, though a younger cat probably wouldn't have jumped from a window six floors up.

That's the trouble with old age, thinks Albert. Your mind starts failing you just when you need it the most.

He isn't at that stage yet, but he wonders how it will be in the years to come: who will be there to stop him wandering the streets in his pyjamas or going for a walk on the railway line. He used to tell himself that Gloria would be a stabilizing influence, but it's hard to claim that now.

Loud voices drift on the air, young men flush with beer. Albert quickens his pace. The streets are already quieter than he would like; a reminder that darkness is a time to lie low.

At moments like this he's glad to be wearing his official

Royal Mail coat, its logo declaring his neutral mission in life, the impartial delivery of post to saints and sinners alike.

Now that retirement is just a few weeks off, he worries whether he'll be allowed to keep the coat – though he also wonders what he's supposed to do with it even if he does. He wants to keep wearing it, of course, but he can see that might lead to all sorts of problems: people haranguing him on the street about lost mail, wanting to know why it took four days for a first-class letter to travel ten miles. He's heard it all in his time. Better, he thinks, just to wear the coat at home sometimes, on Sundays perhaps. But when he imagines the future, it seems every day will feel like a Sunday, so what then?

Gloria miaows, clearly unhappy about, well, everything.

'Look at you. They've turned you into a blunt instrument, haven't they? I could bludgeon someone to death with those legs.'

Encouraged by the thought, he walks a little taller, moving deeper into the warren of graffitied tower blocks and shadowy stairwells that he calls home.

6

IT'S BEEN ALMOST forty years since Albert's wife died, but not much has changed in the flat where they were briefly so happy together. The bed she died in is still here, its mattress springs a little worse for wear, but otherwise functional. The wardrobe where she used to hang her clothes is still in the bedroom, its shelves much less organized than she would have liked. Here and there, a few of her things still remain – a faded glove, a musty scarf – each a bittersweet reminder of a life that has long since vanished.

Perhaps the biggest change is Albert himself: his hair is gently receding, like a slow-moving tide; his once-youthful skin another casualty of age and gravity.

He peers at himself in the mirror, not vain so much as intrigued.

'At least I still have my teeth,' he says to Gloria.

With two broken legs to deal with, she probably doesn't give a shit. While she blinks – in pain, in boredom, it's impossible to tell – Albert bares his teeth and admires them from a variety of angles. He dreams of doing this at the supermarket whenever he buys toothpaste – 'Look, I've still got all my teeth!' he wants to shout, his lips drawn back like a monkey on the attack – but he knows people would think him mad, and who cares if you've got your teeth but lost your mind?

Unaware of finding the thought sad, and unable to see that he's really a man grown old before his years, he turns away from the mirror.

'Well, Gloria, it's time for bed.' He carefully fluffs a mound of shredded toilet roll into a deep nest around her. 'I don't want you worrying about, you know, the call of nature. You just let it out and I'll clean it all up tomorrow.'

He tries to smile as he says it, but he's unsure how this is going to work.

'And I'll sleep with my door open, so you just call if you need me.'

She blinks at him enigmatically and turns to face the window.

She's got a death wish, thinks Albert. She's just biding her time until she can jump again.

While Gloria stares out of the window, Albert looks at a large patch of mould on the wall above, the cause of all his problems. This was the only reason he left the window open today, to let some air in, but all he has to show for it now is a crippled cat and an even bigger patch of mould.

Trying not to worry about it, he simply turns off the light and retreats to his bedroom. Before climbing into bed, he lingers by a photograph of his wife, its tarnished silver frame at risk of disappearing in the chaos of his housekeeping.

'Good night, sweetheart.'

She smiles up at him like a rabbit caught in a car's headlights, trapped between the sixties and the seventies in a strange new world she didn't live long enough to understand.

And then, with the flick of a switch, the day is over.

In darkness now, Albert settles into the furrowed mattress. He's never consciously acknowledged that he's afraid of what each new day might bring; that he's scared of losing what little he has. He just dismisses the sensation as heartburn.

'I really should buy some Tums,' he mutters, as he wraps his arms around a tattered old pillow, shutting his eyes in sleep while the world around him grinds onward in a distant rumble of sirens and car alarms.

And, through it all, Gloria sits immobile in the living room, her legs in plaster but her mind alert, gazing out at the blinking lights of aeroplanes waiting to land at Heathrow and Gatwick.

What she's seen on many occasions but will never comprehend is that the planes are moving in seemingly endless holding patterns, so that it often appears as if some people spend their entire lives trapped, going round and round in circles but never arriving.

LIFE

7

'I THOUGHT YOU'D go to the doctor's together.'

'He decided he'd rather do it alone,' replies Carol, 'but he wants me to meet him afterwards.'

She watches as her best friend Helen pours a cup of herbal tea, the colour as off-putting as the smell. In the background, Kenny G plays on the stereo; a sound well suited to a damp terraced house in Croydon.

'Do you think he'll be okay?' says Helen.

'I don't know. I mean, I hope so.'

'Well, it's nice you still care.'

'Instead of wishing him dead, you mean?'

'It's just, you know, things can get ugly.' She winces as she says it, her own three-year-old divorce still a sore subject. 'And how about you? How are you holding up?'

'Oh, God, I don't know. I'm worried about him, of course, but it all feels a bit like the boy who cried "Wolf" to me. I mean, Bob is the kind of man who gets a cold and thinks he's dying. Give him half an hour on the

Internet and he'll diagnose himself with leukaemia and typhoid.'

'But this is an actual lump?'

'Yes. He even let me feel it.'

Helen's eyes widen, though whether with interest or arousal it's hard to tell. 'And?'

'What can I say? It was a lump. I was just relieved I could touch his balls without him wanting sex too.' Kenny starts playing 'Let It Be'. A line has been crossed. 'Do we have to listen to this bloody music?'

'It's relaxing.'

'Then why do I feel the urge to see him dead?'

'I read that instrumental music is helpful. You know, for stress.'

Carol nods, lets it go for the sake of Helen's nerves. They've known each other since university, and although time has transformed them from two peas in a pod to something more akin to a pea and a turnip, Carol still feels the pod-like comfort of a friendship that's so deep it has no need for a shared taste in music.

Or tea.

She stirs hers, the closest she's willing to come to actually drinking it. In the silence that follows, she decides this is the time for her confession. 'I was going to leave Bob yesterday.'

Helen doesn't look surprised. 'On a Tuesday? That's abstract.'

'What? Is there a commonly accepted day for divorce? Is it more a weekend kind of thing?'

'And presumably you're asking me because I'm so experienced in marital failure.'

'Okay, sorry, that came out wrong.'

'Don't be. I mean, it's true, isn't it?' She looks depressed now, an expression well suited to her hand-knitted sweater, a chunky woollen mass of puce.

'I'd just had such a crap day at work,' says Carol. 'I knew something had to change.'

'You could have just checked the classifieds.'

'But in all likelihood I'd just get another crap job, wouldn't I? I could exchange the mindless paperwork of an insurance company for something equally dull and bureaucratic. And I'd still have to come home to Bob every night. That's the real problem, sharing a life with someone I don't love . . .'

Silence.

'I would have done it this time. I really would.'

'Are you telling me or trying to convince yourself?'

'He's got a lump on his balls! Would you dump a man who's just found a lump on his balls?'

'I'd like to think I wouldn't dump my husband of eighteen years, full stop. There has to be some other way of working through your problems.'

'A gun would probably do it.' She sighs, so distracted she almost drinks her tea. 'As soon as he gets the all-clear, I'm gone.'

She doesn't notice Helen's expression, the fear of a lonely woman in danger of losing her only real friend.

'Where do you think you'll go?'

'I still want to see Athens—' She stops herself, aware

that Helen understands the real meaning of her interest in Athens, a secret they've long agreed is best forgotten. 'And then I don't know,' she adds hurriedly. 'Away from this place.'

'Come on, Croydon's not that bad.'

'Please, it's how Mogadishu would look if it had Burger King and McDonald's.'

The slamming of the front door startles them both. Seconds later, Helen's daughter Jane enters the room with all the grace of a coal miner.

Just one year younger than Sophie, Jane has chosen a different path in life, intentionally flunking all her exams and instead expressing herself in a style best described as Angry Lesbian.

Despite the instrumental music, it's a tense moment. Whereas Carol's relationship with Sophie is defined by a wide intellectual gulf, Helen's problem is much more basic: Jane hates her. It's an obvious contempt, almost electrifying in its intensity, and looking at Helen, Carol can understand why. Despite her self-help books and yoga classes, she's a mess. It's as though divorce has pulled the bathplug from her life and all that's left of her now is some soapy scum clinging to the side of the tub.

'Would you like a cup of tea?' says Helen.

Carol makes a mental note to discuss this with her another time. It doesn't seem very cool to offer any teenager a cup of tea, but especially someone like Jane, who looks like she only wants to sniff glue and die young.

Sure enough, Jane doesn't respond. She simply turns

and leaves the room, the sound of her footsteps on the stairs confirming that she's both angry and overweight.

'It's strange,' says Helen, quietly. 'You always imagine your own child is going to be the sane, successful one; the one with her head screwed on.' She glances up at the ceiling as if she's expecting something else to happen – loud music, perhaps, or the roar of a chain-saw. 'I'm still not sure if she's a dyke or just a scary heterosexual.' She begins chewing a fingernail. 'It'd be interesting to hear what her father thinks, but of course he prefers other people's kids. I call it the here's-one-I-made-earlier approach to family life.'

'Helen, he was a bastard.'

'That's not what his new wife seems to think.'

Carol starts to drink her tea, the only act of sisterhood she can offer right now. She tries not to wince with each sip, even though Helen looks too distracted to notice.

'I suppose she's just at a difficult age,' says Helen. 'Things will probably get better in a year or two.' She doesn't sound as if she believes it, but purely saying it seems to have therapeutic value. 'How's Sophie?'

'Invisible. As ever. Busy being brilliant.'

'An intelligent, sensible daughter. I don't know how you cope.' She tries to smile, but it only makes her look sadder. 'Does she know about Bob?'

'No, we don't want to make her worry. Not that she would.'

'Carol!'

'It's true. She has all the emotion of a laser printer. And yet so certain of her place in the world, so sure she'll get everything she wants.'

'Is that such a bad thing?'

'Oh, fuck knows. Maybe I'm just jealous.' She takes another sip of tea and immediately regrets it. 'I found a picture of myself the other day. Nineteen ninety-three, just graduated, and I thought all things were possible. It was going to be the eighties again, but with better hair and smaller telephones. And there I am, seven months pregnant.' She stares at her cup of tea, the dark, bitter fluid seeming more and more emblematic of her life. 'A shotgun wedding at the age of twenty wasn't quite how I'd imagined things. And it didn't help that I felt like the gun was pointing at me rather than Bob.'

'You could have waited.'

'For what? I mean, let's face it, there's never a good time to marry a man like him. And now . . . now it's already Sophie's turn at being grown-up, and here I am still trying to get it right myself.'

'You know what? You should write a letter.'

'To?'

'It doesn't really matter. The point is you just put down everything you're feeling and then you burn it.'

Carol stares at her, incredulous.

'It's a letter to the universe,' adds Helen, as if this explains everything. 'It's a ritual.'

'If I'm going to the trouble of telling someone what I think, would it not be better to actually send it to them?'

'No, it's too confrontational. That's not how the universe works.'

'What about the comet that wiped out the dinosaurs? That

seems pretty confrontational.' She waits for a response, but it's obvious Helen is ignoring her. 'Anyway, you know me, I've spent most of my life not saying what I think. I should start being more confrontational, not less.'

'That might be difficult if Bob's lump is bad news.'

'It's nothing.' It comes out harshly, more a rebuke than a reply.

Helen sips her tea, clearly aware that she's just touched a nerve. 'Well, I hope for his sake you're right.'

The agreement is that Carol will meet Bob on the high street. Near the doctor's surgery, but not so near that it feels like she's waiting for him to come out – even though she is – because in Bob's mind this implies something bad. He'd explained this in great detail over breakfast.

'People only hang around the doctor's when somebody's dying.'

'I don't think anyone dies at the doctor's, Bob.'

'Hospitals, then.'

'What about people giving birth? People hang around outside for that.'

Bob had responded to that comment with an angry look, the inviolable rectitude of being the one with the lump.

Thinking it best to accommodate his whims, Carol arrives at the agreed time – positioning herself within range of the doctor's surgery but certainly not close enough to send Bob to an early grave – and she waits.

And waits.

As boredom sets in, she wanders over to a travel agency,

begins to browse the offers in the window. These aren't just flights and package holidays, they're invitations to escape and reinvent, to have another go at being happy.

In the early days when she used to think of leaving Bob, Sophie was always part of the fantasy: the two of them going away together, discovering all that was really missing in their relationship was a sandy beach and constant sunshine. Yet something has changed as the years have passed. Despite Carol's best intentions to learn from her own mother's mistakes, she and Sophie now stand on opposing sides of a wide emotional gulf. And, yes, there are times when she believes she can dive in and swim to the other side, all her years of frustrated motherhood exorcized in the simple act of reaching out. But more often, as she imagines standing there gazing across at the silhouette of her daughter, she can see herself giving up, walking away from a relationship that ceased to make sense years ago.

If Carol heard another parent say that, she'd be the first to judge, and yet this is her truth – her dark, shameful secret.

Before she's even aware of what she's doing, she's hurried into a corner shop and bought a cheap notepad. Going back outside, she takes a seat on a vandalized bench and starts to write.

Dear Universe,
    I don't like my daughter.

She stares at the words, then crosses them out with such force she tears through the paper.

'Shit.'

She hesitates over the page, its ink-stained tatters a fitting testament to her mental state.

Taking a deep breath, she begins to write again.

I am a bad mother. I would like to think this isn't entirely my own fault. I mean, had I given birth to a child rather than an encyclopedia, maybe things would have worked out differently.

She hesitates, can feel what's coming next.

Of course, things might have been better if I hadn't fallen in love with another man. Or if I'd had the courage to spend my life with him rather than Bob.

She freezes over the words, dazed at the enormity of what she's just written, her breathing fast and shallow now.

This isn't a letter, it's a bomb. It's too much, too soon. She'd never planned to actually burn it but, looking at it now, she can think of nothing else she'd rather do. She certainly can't keep it in her bag. It doesn't even seem safe to throw it in the bin: she couldn't sleep at night knowing those words are out there, somewhere, anywhere.

She rushes back into the corner shop and buys a cigarette lighter with all the fraught, nervous urgency of a chronic nicotine addict. Even the elderly Punjabi man behind the till seems alarmed – a man who's probably seen it all in his time, riots and looting and worse, and yet still, on a quiet afternoon in Croydon, Carol is able to unnerve him.

Back out on the street, she hurries to a bin, unaware that a nurse is now standing in the entrance of the doctor's surgery watching her every move.

Her hands trembling, Carol tears the page from her notepad, and rips out several pages beneath it just for good measure. She holds them all over the flame, a gentle breeze making the job harder than she'd expected.

Finally the pages catch light, the fire engulfing them so quickly that Carol drops them with a start. She peers into the bin, desperately hoping the fire will burn itself out, but the pages sit atop a virtual tinderbox of old newspapers and greasy fast-food packaging. Within seconds, flames lick from the top of the bin and a thick pall of smoke begins to rise into the air.

Carol scurries away, glancing around to make sure no one has noticed.

Which is when she sees the nurse.

'Excuse me,' the nurse calls. 'Are you Mrs Cooper by any chance?'

Carol considers running off, but then decides against it. Much better, she thinks, to approach with a calm and collected air. She isn't the kind of woman who could start an inferno. The nurse is simply overworked. It's a trick of the light.

As she gets nearer, she can see the nurse's eyes flitting back and forth between her and the thick cloud of smoke now rolling down the street.

'Is something wrong?' says Carol.

'It's about your husband.' The nurse lowers her voice. 'I think it's better if we talk inside.'

8

ALBERT STICKS HIS fork deeper into the toaster, still unable to get the bread out. It doesn't occur to him to unplug it first. That's the thing about getting older: it isn't forgetfulness, it's just that lots of things cease to be important. He's survived with these habits for decades, so why start worrying now?

'There,' he says, as he pulls out a charred slice of toast. 'It's a little overdone, but that just adds flavour.'

He carries it through to the living room, his mind busy with what to say to Darren. In simple terms, he needs to take some time off, but he's never tried asking for it at such short notice.

'Yes, Darren? It's Albert.' He holds an imaginary phone in his hand, tries to sound confident and yet deferential. 'Yes, I need to go and see the council. About a damp patch. I'll only be an hour or two, then I'll rush straight in.' He turns to Gloria, now sitting regally on a freshly cleaned bed. 'That sounds reasonable, surely?'

She ignores him, her full attention on the window.

'Though I don't know why I'm worrying. The closer I get to retiring, the less anyone seems to care what I do.' It hurts to say it, but it's true. It's got to the stage where he suspects he could go missing for days – perhaps even die in the staff room, a desiccated corpse wedged in one of the coffee-stained armchairs – and no one would notice.

Even after he's steeled himself for the call, it doesn't work out the way he'd planned.

'Why not take the whole day?' says Darren.

'But I don't need to.'

'We can call it a sick day.'

'But I'm not sick.'

'Well, it wouldn't be much fun taking the day off if you were feeling ill, would it?'

'Well, no . . .'

'See? Problem solved.'

'It's just I left the windows open yesterday because of the damp and Gloria went and jumped, can you believe it? Six floors down. She was lucky to survive.'

There's a long, confused silence at the other end of the line.

'Gloria's my cat.'

'Ah, I see.'

'She's got two legs in—'

'You have a lovely day off, okay?'

'Oh, all ri—'

Darren hangs up.

'Well,' says Albert to Gloria, 'that went okay, didn't it?'

He glances up at the mouldy patch, certain it's grown in

the last few hours. It's obvious the window should stay open while he's out, but there's Gloria to think of. Admittedly her front legs are now encased in plaster, but where there's a will . . .

Not wanting to take any chances, he ties a length of string around her neck, then fastens the other end to one of the table legs. 'There. Better safe than sorry, eh?'

The council office has the kind of harsh strip lighting that manages to make everyone look ill and yet still leaves the space feeling dim. There's an almost palpable sense of despair, too, as if some of the people in the queue have been waiting there months, maybe years. Even the staff appear depressed, so that whenever one of them leaves the room it's impossible to tell if they've gone to get something or to shoot themselves.

When Albert's turn eventually comes, nothing is as simple as it should be. It isn't that he'd expected it to be easy – this is the council, after all – he just hadn't expected the experience to be so predatory.

'And you live alone?' says the woman behind the desk.

'That's right.'

She begins to tap a pen against her keyboard; an excitable *tap, tap, tap*, like she's just had a brilliant idea.

'And you're happy there?'

'It's full of memories from when my wife was alive. I wouldn't give it up for all the tea in China.'

'But it's a bit big for one person, don't you think?'

'It's only got one bedroom.'

'Yeah, but it's a bedroom for two.'

'Look, I only want the damp fixed.'

'And there's a long waiting list for that kind of thing. It might take . . .' She glances at her computer and shrugs, as though technology has no way of understanding what goes on in government. 'It might be better if you thought about moving to a new place.'

'But that won't actually fix the problem, will it?'

'But it'll become someone else's problem.'

'Only if you give the flat to someone else.'

'Well, it can't sit empty. There's a long waiting list.'

'Wouldn't you have to fix the damp problem first?'

'Of course.'

'So why can't you try while I'm there?'

She leans forward and starts to speak in a loud, slow voice. 'There's a long waiting list, which is why we prioritize the empty flats.'

'So what you're saying is you can't fix my place because I'm living there?'

'Yes, exactly.'

For a split second, Albert wonders what would happen if he was a violent man. 'Maybe I'll just have a go at fixing it myself,' he says, with a polite smile.

'I still think you should consider moving. I'm sure we could find you something newer, cosier.'

'No, thank you.'

'Then you should at least keep us informed about that damp problem,' she says, as he stands up. 'If it gets any worse we might have to declare the flat a health risk.'

*

Two hours in the council office should have been enough to prepare Albert for anything – water-boarding, for instance, or a slow, painful death – but when he gets home and sees his neighbour outside, his heart sinks.

In theory, Max Davis is only watering his many potted plants; a harmless seventy-year-old doddering about in the sunshine. In reality, he's spoiling for a fight, and will stay outside until he's tasted blood. Usually Albert's.

'Shouldn't you be at work?' he says, as Albert approaches.

'I'm checking on Gloria.' Albert immediately regrets justifying himself. This is the problem with Max: they've known each other since way back and somehow their teenage pecking order has remained intact through the decades, so that to ignore him seems unnatural, even dangerous.

'I hope you're bringing it a parachute,' says Max, as he grabs at Albert's shopping bag and peers inside – nothing to see but a tub of putty and a bottle of disinfectant. Albert pulls the bag free and strides towards his front door.

'Still,' says Max, 'that cat's better out the window than out here.' He glances at his potted plants, less with affection than ownership. 'If I saw that cat messing with my flowers, I'd chuck it over the edge myself.'

'Why would a cat want to touch your flowers?'

'What are you talking about? Cats love flowers. Don't you even know that? You've got a cat, for Christ's sake, and you don't even know that?' He laughs, clearly satisfied with how the day is turning out. 'With a mind as sharp as yours, Albert, it's no wonder you've stuck with the Post Office all these years.'

9

Bob has never been very good at hearing bad news, but Carol can't recall him locking himself in a toilet before.

'Bob, it's all right. Just open the door, okay?'

'I want to stay in here for a while.'

'It's a toilet, Bob. You'll be more comfortable at home.'

'Just for a while.'

Aware that at least three people in the waiting room are listening to their conversation, Carol retreats.

'He seemed quite composed when he went in,' explains the nurse. 'The hysterical ones are normally much easier to spot.'

Dr Singh approaches them, his face a picture of unconcern. 'How is he?' he says, in a soft Indian burr, so that for a moment Carol thinks he's asking the nurse what she thinks of her.

'He's talking,' the nurse replies.

Dr Singh nods. This is evidently a good sign.

'I told your husband he needs to see a specialist,' he says

matter-of-factly. 'I did not think this alone would provoke a panic attack.'

It's hard to tell if he's impressed or disappointed that Bob has defied his expectations, all his years of training turned on their head by an overly emotional man locked in a toilet.

'So you think it's serious?' says Carol.

Dr Singh shrugs. 'It's not really my field, but certainly, if my testicle felt like his, I'd be worried, yes.'

Carol and the nurse stand in an awkward silence, neither of them wanting to think about Dr Singh's nuts.

From outside, the distant sound of a fire-engine siren steadily grow louder.

'I encouraged your husband to take a philosophical view,' says Dr Singh. 'At this stage, possibly the worst-case scenario is simply that the testicle will be removed, in which case we replace it with a silicone sack of equal weight, so the overall . . .' He hesitates over the right word, then gestures with a clenched fist. 'The overall *sensation* remains the same. It's really quite a simple procedure. There'll be some pain and discomfort, of course, and a certain amount of humiliation, I suppose, but I told him, even with just the one testicle, he must still try and take these things like a man.'

Carol can begin to understand Bob's panic. She wouldn't be surprised if the doctor had offered to do it there and then with his letter-opener. 'I don't understand your concern,' she can imagine him saying, 'the testicles bleed heavily, it's true, but it won't take long. Just a quick slit and a sharp yank.'

'If you don't mind,' she says, 'I think I'll try again.'

She goes back to the toilet door and knocks gently. 'Bob,

I'm going to take you home now, okay? I don't want you staying here.'

The siren grows to a deafening crescendo and then abruptly cuts dead, the fire engine obviously parked nearby.

'Bob?'

'Your mum called.'

'What?'

'Your mum called yesterday. Said she can never get you on your mobile.'

'Bob, that doesn't mat—'

'I forgot to tell you.'

'It doesn't matter, Bob. Really.'

'You only say that because you hate her.'

Carol glances back at the nurse and Dr Singh, aware that they are also listening. 'Bob, I don't hate her. And it wouldn't matter even if I did, okay? I just want to get you home, make you comfortable.' She flails for something more to say. 'We can watch some *Doctor Who*.' Still nothing. 'And there's a nice dessert in the fridge.'

Moments later, the door clicks open in a haze of pine-scented air-freshener.

'What kind of dessert?'

10

GLORIA HASN'T MOVED while Albert was out. Which makes sense, really, considering half her limbs are encased in plaster. There's something about the scene – a cat lying on the living-room floor, half crippled, tied to the dining table with coarse string – that reminds Albert of RSPCA posters. *'Stamp out animal cruelty. Donate now!'*

Deciding he may have overestimated her motor skills, he unties her. 'There, does that feel better?'

Even he realizes this is a stupid question: with two legs in plaster, a piece of string around her neck is really the least of her problems.

'I'm going to fix the wall. You can watch me if you like.' He thinks about what Max said. 'And if you're a good girl, I'll buy you some flowers one of these days. Would you like that?' She stares at him as he opens the window. 'I would have got you some sooner,' he adds, under his breath, 'but I'm not a bloody mind-reader.'

Under Gloria's steady gaze, he leans out to get a better

view of the wall. A big crack in the façade roughly matches the location of the mouldy patch.

'That's it, all right.' As he peers down at the six-storey drop below, his heart skips a beat. 'Well . . . that's a long way down. Though, of course, you'd know all about that.'

Not wanting to look scared in front of Gloria, he loads a spatula with putty and climbs out onto the window ledge.

'It's just the arthritis,' he says, as his legs begin to shake. 'I'm not as young as I used to be.'

Clutching the window frame with one hand, he leans across and spreads a thick smear over the crack; it's not enough to fix the problem, but it's a good start.

He scrambles back indoors, his heart racing. 'Well, this isn't so hard, is it?'

His legs still shaking, he picks up the string and ties it around Gloria's neck again. He then takes the other end from the table leg and knots it around one of his belt loops.

'It's not like I think anything bad's going to happen, but if it does, at least I'll know you're taken care of.' He takes her widening eyes as a sign of approval. 'Yes, that's right. I love you too.'

Ten minutes later and the exterior wall is a festering mess of putty smeared on in haphazard spatula strokes and greasy finger marks. It isn't pretty, but neither is the building so it really doesn't seem to matter.

Saved from a tandem base jump with Albert, Gloria watches as he now stands on a chair and tackles the living-room wall. With each wipe of disinfectant, the mould transforms into a thin green stain, the paint beneath beginning to dissolve in the chemical onslaught. After just a few wipes, the wall looks considerably worse than it has at any time in its forty-year history.

'Well, at least the furry stuff has gone, which is probably all that matters.'

He gets off the chair and takes a few steps back, hoping the wall might look better from a distance. It doesn't.

'Well, look!' he says, eager to change the subject. 'It's barely one o'clock!'

There was a time when this kind of statement would have had him rushing back to work, but that was when people still wanted him to. Even Albert can see that things have changed now. The world has moved on without him, and he just has to muddle through as best he can.

He stands there in the middle of the room, suddenly aware that the day feels silent and empty.

'So,' he says quietly, 'I suppose this is what retirement will be like . . .'

11

Carol expects to see a change in Bob when she gets him home. Not a lift in spirits, of course, but *something* – an outpouring of his darkest fears, perhaps, or some kind of manic episode in which he loudly plays all his Fleetwood Mac albums back to back. Instead she gets silence. It's apparent from the way he skulks about the house that he wants her to be within sight at all times, and yet still he says nothing. There's something unnerving about it; a mental breakdown that hasn't yet decided what it wants to be. Carol can imagine he might spring to life at any moment and start smashing things or try to take his ear off with one of their Ikea knives.

'Is there something wrong?' says Sophie, as she scours the kitchen cupboards for food. Her words express concern, but the tone does not: it sounds more like irritation that her parents' problems are threatening to intrude on her own happiness.

It's obvious Bob is struggling to find a diplomatic

response, possibly struggling to put together any kind of sentence at all.

'We're fine,' says Carol.

Sophie shoots her an angry glance. 'God, what are you, his mother?' Carol wants to say, yes, that's often what I feel like, but Sophie is already heading for the front door. 'If you're both going to act like this, I'd rather be elsewhere.'

Moments later she's gone, the world immediately seeming a better place.

'Teenagers . . .' says Carol, but Bob doesn't appear to be listening. Instead, he's wedged himself into a corner of the kitchen and is now staring at the spice rack.

The phone begins to ring, its sound echoing through the silent house. Leaving Bob to meditate over the dried basil, Carol rushes into the living room and snatches it up.

'Hello?' Her face sinks. 'Mum . . . No, why would there be something wrong?'

She watches as Bob appears in the doorway, his shoulders hunched as though his whole body is on the verge of structural collapse.

'No, no,' she says breezily, 'we're all fine. Sophie's out. And Bob and I . . . we both had the day off work, thought we'd take advantage of the weather.' She then remembers the day was actually cold and grey. 'I mean, who knows how long before winter really sets in?'

The conversation continues for a few more minutes, Carol deflecting each of her mother's comments with increasing disinterest – the jaded manner of a tennis pro who's lost her passion for the game.

'Well, I'll pop over next week some time,' she says, in lieu of goodbye, and hangs up.

In the silence that follows, Bob at last speaks. 'The dessert in the fridge looks lovely. Did you really get it just to make me feel better?'

'Er, yes.'

He begins to cry. 'I don't deserve you.'

Before Carol can agree, Bob is sliding down the doorframe, his legs crumpling beneath him.

She goes to his side, at first just squeezing his shoulder in a chummy approximation of intimacy. 'Bob, it's going to be all right. We'll get through this, okay?'

He curls up on the floor, shuddering as he tries to hide his tear-stained face from view.

'Look, come here . . .' She sits down beside him and takes him in her arms, instinctively reverting to her role as the wife and mother who fixes everyone else's problems even when she can't fix her own.

As she holds him close, the two of them rocking back and forth, she quietly gives thanks that the threat of cancer has all but killed his sex drive; that she can comfort him without worrying that a simple hug will escalate into an unwanted sympathy-fuck.

And then she hears the other man's voice. A memory she can suppress but not exorcize. A memory that has survived the years intact when so much else has not.

'You don't have to go back to him tonight,' the voice says. 'You can stay with me if you want.'

It feels as if he's whispering the words in her ear right now. His lips just inches from the back of her neck.

Just as she did all those years ago, she imagines that, yes, she will stay with him. She will choose her own happiness over Bob's and everything else will just have to work itself out. And for a brief moment, the pain of that memory burns so clearly that she too begins to cry.

12

FOR THE LAST forty years, Albert's night-time ritual has been to watch television. Or not to watch it, but rather sit in front of it. It doesn't much matter to him what's on, because it's all bullshit anyway, the crime dramas and naff talent contests only echoing the violence and mediocrity of everyday life. He just sits there every night, grateful for the company.

Having spent his entire life handling mail, he's always imagined other people spend their evenings reading and rereading letters from children and dear friends, giggling over their favourite lines and fussing over long and heartfelt replies.

He glances over at the mail he's received that day, all of it junk. As he's never owned a home, the glossy flyers offering generous home-equity loans seem specifically designed to make him feel like a non-person, the wrong sort of retiree. *'Congratulations on making it to this age. Too bad you got it all wrong.'*

That's not to say he never gets personal mail. There are

occasional cards from an old friend in Australia, but even they contain nothing but talk of blue skies and grandchildren, and are always written with a slightly dutiful air, the words making their friendship feel more like an obligation.

For a while, after Albert's wife died, those friendships had become intense and cosseting, almost suffocating in their care and concern. Then they began to fade away, as if all the effort had burned them out. For Albert, it was rather like being in a room when a light-bulb blows. For a brief moment, his friendships had burned bright, and then he found himself sitting alone in the dark.

'We might have emigrated, mightn't we?'

Gloria glances up at him, but quickly looks away again. It's obvious he's speaking to that other presence in the room.

'If Harry and his wife could stay together for fifty years, imagine how well we would have done. They've always been such a miserable pair.'

He smiles to himself, happy that he can still talk to her like this; that he can still feel her even after all these years. She's a phantom limb, gone but ever present. And the older he gets, the less it seems to matter that he's sitting alone talking to himself, the memory of her becoming clearer even as everything around him begins to blur.

In the slow-motion meltdown of Carol's week, the decision to take a few more days off work is the least of her concerns.

'I didn't feel like explaining Bob's lump. It just seemed easier to tell them *I'm* sick,' she says to Helen, as they walk through the park, each of them wrapped up against the chill autumn air. 'They didn't even ask any questions. It was like I'd told them something they'd known for years.'

'How's Bob coping?'

'Badly. But I could have said the same thing about the World Cup. Bob's not really a coper. Fortunately he has World of Warcraft to keep him occupied – my eternal man-child.'

'And how are you doing?'

'Oh, me . . . I'm just doing what I always seem to do. Helping him keep things together.'

'Which is the right thing to do on this occasion.'

'Unlike the last eighteen years, you mean?' Helen doesn't respond. 'I was awake half the night with this image in my head. Bob was in the *Daily Mail* talking about his thirty-year fight with cancer and how he couldn't have done it without my support. And I was right there in the background, doubled over from carrying his dinner to him on a tray and emptying his bed pans, all the while thinking, Die, fuck it, die!'

Passers-by look askance, but Carol doesn't notice.

'Then I think how much he needs me right now . . . Leaving him would be like abandoning a puppy on the motorway.'

Saddened by the thought, she doesn't notice a young man jog past with an athletic, self-assured swagger, the drape of his clothes suggesting a lean, muscled physique. For Helen, however, he's clearly some kind of catnip.

'I just want passion,' says Carol, oblivious to Helen's lust. 'I want Heathcliff and *Wuthering Heights*.'

'Then read the book. Get the DVD.' She turns to watch the jogger, his muscled legs propelling him on and on, out of her life.

'I always thought I'd spend my thirties fussing over organic vegetables and dinner parties full of interesting people.'

'Organic stuff is just so expensive . . .' Helen looks depressed now – depressed that the jogger didn't turn to look at her too; didn't stop running altogether and take her right there in the park, on the children's swings and against the damp bark of the oak trees.

The sound of Carol's voice reels her in. 'I was thinking of Richard last night.'

'I was waiting to hear that name,' says Helen. 'As soon

as you mentioned Athens the other day, I knew it was only a matter of time.'

'I know you don't approve—'

'Richard was a long time ago. He was just a fling.'

'So was Bob, but look at us now.'

'Still, it doesn't help.'

'Maybe I just want to know where he's gone.'

'And how would it make this situation any better for you or for Bob? Richard's not in your life any more. That's surely as much as you need to know.' Evidently uncomfortable playing the role of bad cop, she softens her tone. 'See, this is why you should write a letter to the universe. You've got all this stuff on your mind. Sometimes you just need to get it out there, get it off your chest.'

She sounds so convincing on the subject that Carol has to remind herself this is the woman who once went through a phase of drinking her own urine. Even now Carol is careful about what she drinks from Helen's fridge.

'Well, I'll think about it,' she says.

'I think we both know what that means.'

'No, really,' she replies, already certain she'll never try writing a letter again. 'Just give me some time.'

14

'I HEARD YOU were sick.'

'Not really,' says Albert. 'It was just a day off.'

His colleague Mickey Wong appears to consider the words. 'So you were skiving, then?'

'Well, no. It was Darren's suggestion.'

'Oh, of course it was. That wanker! It's another form of corruption when you think about it. Everyone abusing the system for their own pleasure. This place is rotten to the core. The whole country, really.'

It strikes Albert as a little heavy-handed that one dubious sick day – his first in forty years – can be used as an indictment of the entire nation, but that's the kind of person Mickey is.

In appearance, he's the archetypal Chinaman, a pint-sized version of Chairman Mao. As soon as he opens his mouth, however, it's the streets of London that come rushing out. In fact, to listen to him with your eyes closed is to find yourself in the wrong part of Hackney, desperate for a policeman or an empty cab.

Mickey's preferred topics of conversation don't help. You could say he specializes in brutal honesty and offence, always served with a blithe unawareness of everyone else's feelings. In that respect, a conversation with him isn't so much a gentle to-and-fro as a random onslaught, the verbal equivalent of being mown down by automatic gunfire.

'But there's no need to feel bad about bunking off,' he says to Albert. 'I mean, what are you? A mere cog in a big fucking machine. A machine that never cared about you in the first place. And now you're retiring, forget about it. You're nothing. Less than nothing.'

Albert tries to remind himself this is Mickey's way of being supportive. 'Call me mad,' he says, 'but I'm still going to miss this place.'

'But nobody here's going to miss *you*, are they? That's what's tragic about it. I mean, they just think you're old and useless, so you can sod off. It's not even as if you have anything to do any more, is it? You just come in and try to look busy.'

Although this is true, Albert still feels the need to protest. 'I have things to do.'

'Bollocks you do! Shaking your willy in the Gents doesn't count. But it's their fault, Albert, not yours. That's why I say they're all cunts, the lot of them. And now this talk of privatization. You can bet that's going to fuck us all up the arse!' He gazes around the room as if he can already see the place in ruins. 'Mark my words, Albert, you're getting your pension just in time. Maybe there won't even be a pension by the time I retire.'

'Do you really think so?'

'What do you care? You'll be dead by then.'

Darren appears from nowhere, cutting between them with a Teflon smile. 'Albert, I've got a special task for you.'

'If he wants a blow-job,' says Mickey, loudly, 'remember to use your teeth.'

There are a few seconds of stilted silence, Darren's management training obviously never having prepared him for moments like this.

He forces another smile. 'Albert, if you'll follow me . . .'

He leads Albert away from the main work area, the building becoming quieter with every step.

They finally enter a small room full of dusty mail sacks. Up near the ceiling is one small window, the glass dirty and barred, the view of nothing but grey, wet sky.

'The undeliverable mail,' says Albert. 'This lot's nothing but rubbish.'

'No, Albert, this is a . . . a Mail Redirection Facility.' He says it without a hint of irony, even though the only redirection from here is to the nearest bonfire. 'I thought you could spend your final weeks keeping on top of things.'

'On top of what?'

'Well, look at it. It's a bit messy for a start. And there are the letters to Santa. We ought to start saving a few of those. You know,' he adds, with a wink, 'sending them on to the North Pole. Might look a bit suspicious if Santa's ignoring all the kids in our district.'

'Don't see why. Most of them are cheeky bastards.'

'The point is, we've neglected this room for too long. Getting it in order can be your crowning triumph.'

'So I get it all straight, and then it gets chucked?'

'Destroyed, Albert. For the senders' privacy.' He hesitates, clearly aware that this still doesn't answer the question. 'Royal Mail has standards, Albert. You of all people know that. For as long as these letters are here with us, they need to be . . . managed.' He looks at his watch. 'Look, I'm running late for a meeting, but you let me know if there's anything you need, all right?'

He leaves the room, the sound of his footsteps fading into a silence that Albert knows only too well.

15

Bob's specialist appointment eventually takes place on a Friday afternoon, providing a grim prognosis perfectly timed to ruin the whole weekend.

'They're talking about surgery next week,' he says.

'Well, better out than in,' replies Carol. This immediately strikes her as the wrong thing to say. Even Bob appears to find the comment insensitive. 'I mean, if there's a problem, then, you know, you need to get rid of it.'

Frankly, there's still something strained in these discussions. Even after eighteen years of marriage, a period that has included occasional sex, neither of them feels comfortable talking about his testicles. And now that Bob's nuts have become the centrepiece of their lives, every conversation is mired in mutual embarrassment.

'Apparently, it's a very straightforward process,' he says.

'I would think so.'

'I'll be home the next day. And even with, you know, just the one, I'll still be fertile.'

Carol has no idea what she's supposed to say to this. In as much as she avoids sex with Bob whenever possible, he was really rendered infertile years ago. Even if she actually loved him, it would be hard to imagine her wanting another child at the age of thirty-eight: an opportunity to fuck up her forties and fifties too.

And what would Sophie make of a younger sibling? she wonders. She can picture her resenting it, indoctrinating it, even killing it, but the idea of familial harmony draws a total blank.

She realizes Bob is staring at her, evidently in need of reassurance that his plane can still fly on one engine. 'Well . . . great,' she says, aware that she should probably add something else, but unsure what. 'If ever I want to get pregnant, I'll know where to come.'

As tributes to masculine prowess go, it isn't much, but she knows men like Bob have to take compliments wherever they can find them. It isn't as if he has spent his life being admired and desired by the opposite sex – or the same sex, as far as she's aware; Carol doesn't have any gay friends, but she's pretty certain the average gay man wouldn't want to jerk off over Bob's picture.

'So what do you want to do this weekend?' says Bob.

'No, it should be me asking you that question.'

Bob has clearly been expecting her to say this. They both know it's his day, his week, possibly even a lot more than that.

'Whatever you want to do is fine,' says Carol. 'This whole weekend is about you.'

By the time Monday morning rolls around, it would take nuclear devastation to keep Carol away from the office. She would happily walk there barefoot over the smouldering ruins of London, purely for the pleasure of getting away from Bob.

Without enough facts to draw the charitable conclusion, Sophie had inevitably decided her parents were acting like sad losers and had promptly gone to stay at a friend's house for a couple of days. Alone with Bob and undisturbed by the usual to and fro of family life, Carol's entire weekend had spiralled down into a maudlin experience of musical navel-gazing, a process that involved lots of Kate Bush videos on YouTube – each of them watched numerous times – and hours spent reminiscing over a musty collection of music-festival wristbands.

Until now, Carol had never thought of Kate Bush as symptomatic of a mental problem, but Bob had managed to change that for ever. He'd become particularly emotional on the fourth replay of 'Army Dreamers'.

'They should play this outside the army recruitment offices,' he said. 'She was telling us about Iraq and we wouldn't listen.'

'Bob, it was nineteen eighty-three.'

'But she could see it coming. Listen to her.'

As for the festival wristbands, a little humour might have lightened the mood; for Carol they weren't reminders of music so much as mud, long queues for stinking toilets and endless traffic jams. Bob, however, had conveniently rewritten history so that each wristband became a mawkish tribute to better, happier, more innocent times.

'That was one of the best moments of my life,' he said, about one of many forgettable performances. 'I think that band was probably the best thing to come out of the nineties.'

Carol wanted to point out that the band hadn't actually come out of the nineties: it had sunk from view along with the decade itself and its members could probably now be found working in Tesco and B&Q.

Little wonder, then, that she'd literally leaped from bed on Monday morning.

'It's not even seven,' says Bob, as she bustles downstairs, already dressed and ready to go.

'I've got lots to catch up on.'

'At least have breakfast first.'

'I'll grab something on the way.'

She suddenly realizes that Bob, the probable cancer patient, is standing in the hallway looking lost.

She stops and tries to sound concerned. 'Will you be okay?' *As if I give a fuck.*

'Yeah,' he replies forlornly. 'I'll be fine.'

She gives him a quick kiss on the forehead – as sexual as Florence Nightingale on a TB ward – and rushes from the house.

Carol's enthusiasm for the office evaporates as soon as she arrives. In many ways, its bright lights and sterile furniture are logical extensions of her home life, so that it begins to feel like she's still stuck with Bob, albeit in a different shape and form. There's Bob the uncomfortable chair. And Bob the desk that's the wrong height. On the far side of the room, there's Bob the photocopier that either jams or spits out crooked copies, or both. And, of course, who could forget the office mascot, Bob the jar of instant coffee?

'You're in bright and early,' says Cynthia, whose desk is immediately next to Carol's.

'You know me,' replies Carol, 'Monday mornings and all.'

Cynthia sits down at her desk and begins the elaborate process of eating a muffin: slowly peeling away its wrapper in a way that strikes Carol as vaguely sexual, as though she's preparing to do something other than put it in her mouth.

'That's not much for breakfast,' says Carol.

'It's not,' replies Cynthia, as she takes her first bite. 'It's a post-breakfast snack. To keep my energy up.'

Weighing well over three hundred pounds, it's very likely that Cynthia needs more energy than most just to walk to the toilet, possibly even to sit still and breathe.

Despite the alarming nature of her obesity, she's known to be very defensive about her size. 'Everyone in my family is like this,' is her usual response.

'That's because you're all greedy bastards,' someone once replied. He was assigned to a different office the same day.

Ever since, Carol and her colleagues have been careful not to say anything about Cynthia's weight. They simply watch as she eats her way through each day, growing larger and larger by the month. Carol wonders how it will all end. Whether political correctness will demand the company eventually invest in a crane to hoist her up the outside of the building. And whether everyone will be given protective clothing for the moment when she explodes.

'So where were you last week?' says Cynthia, as she pulls another muffin from her bag.

'My husband was sick.' This feels like such a flat response, so unworthy of the drama she's lived through for the last five days. 'It's his testicle. They think it might be cancer.'

'Fuck, that's heavy.' Evidently tired of the muffin foreplay, she just rips away the wrapper and takes a big bite. 'I don't know what I'd do if it was my husband,' she adds, spitting crumbs on her keyboard as she speaks.

Carol knows that Cynthia will never find herself in this position – if her husband looks anything like her, he presumably hasn't been able to see or feel his balls for decades. Anyway, he'd be dead of something else long before the cancer caught up with him. 'We're just taking it one day at a time.'

'Life,' Cynthia replies at length. 'It's all bollocks!' She begins to laugh at her own joke, her mouth still full.

Aware that Cynthia might choke on her muffin at any second, Carol decides to go and make a cup of coffee – if the worst happens, it seems easier and kinder just to let her die.

The rest of the day is spent in a haze of inane tasks, so that by mid-afternoon Carol really can't decide which is worse: coming to the office or going home.

Then Bob calls.

'It's good news,' he says. 'Well, sort of. At the very least, it's not bad news. I mean, under the circumstances, bad news would have to be really bad news, and this definitely isn't.'

'Bob, what are you trying to say?' It comes out so harshly, he audibly deflates.

'I'm going to see a new specialist.'

'Okay . . .' she says, expecting him to elaborate.

Nothing.

'Why?'

'My boss thinks I should get a second opinion. On the company medical. The private one.' He says it proudly, like he's just been given a promotion rather than the opportunity to have a testicle removed by Bupa.

'He told me to take as much time as I want and to see as many specialists as it takes.'

It's a kind offer, but it also sounds like a convenient way of keeping him out of the office – 'Why just get one or two opinions when you can get ten, twenty?' Specialists could tell him he needs both legs amputated, maybe a kidney transplant too, and the company would probably be there to egg him on, all for the pleasure of not having him around for a while longer.

'. . . so that'll be tomorrow afternoon,' Bob is saying, though Carol has lost track of what he's talking about. 'And then we'll see.'

'Yes,' she replies, as patiently as she can. 'Yes, we will.'

What she wants to tell him is to just get on with it: to have the testicle removed so he can get on with his life and she can get on with hers. It's the first flush of an anger that feels frightening in its intensity. She knows if she says another word, years of pent-up frustration will come bursting to the surface and cancer will quickly come to be the least of Bob's worries.

She forces the kindest voice she can: 'Look, Bob, I'm in the middle of something right now . . .'

'Oh, not to worry. I ought to be giving my new specialist a call. You know, the *private* one.'

In the seconds after he hangs up, Carol sits there with the phone still in her hand, aware that she is about to do something completely out of character, but still not sure what. She can imagine standing up at her desk and shouting, 'FUCK,' very, very loudly. She can just as easily see herself smashing the telephone into a million pieces, stomping on the plastic fragments until she's worn a hole in the carpet.

Instead she does something completely unexpected.

She reaches for a blank sheet of paper and begins to write.

Thirty minutes later, Carol certainly looks happier. She seals the envelope with a satisfaction she hasn't felt in a long time.

Setting fire to it is out of the question. She could try it again in the privacy of her own home, but life is already bad enough without burning down the house too.

'I'm just popping out for a moment,' she says to Cynthia, who replies with a nod – a gesture that surely requires extraordinary effort – and goes back to grazing on a bag of M&Ms.

Carol walks out to the lift with a growing sense of excitement. She already knows what she's going to do, but even she can't quite believe it.

As she comes out to the street, she thinks of people who

pray; who feel better not just because they've said what's on their minds, but also because they think they've been heard. Does it matter if they really are? Not especially, she decides. It's the mere possibility that counts.

She stops in front of a post box, her heart racing. With a shaky hand, she draws a smiley face in the top right-hand corner of the envelope and drops it in.

And sure enough, as she hears her letter fall to the bottom, she does feel better.

16

ALBERT'S FIRST DAY in his new job is dedicated to making the room look tidier, a process that involves lots of long tea breaks.

After a weekend in which he began to dread returning to work, he spends Monday trying to organize the mail – filtering out the letters to Santa Claus, for instance. He finds lots of letters to God as well, as if the postal service has long solved life's greatest mystery: while the rest of the world debates God's existence, Royal Mail not only knows the answer, it has His home address.

'Crackpots, the lot of them,' mutters Albert, as he files the letters in the bin.

By Tuesday he's beginning to read some of the mail. Strictly speaking this isn't part of the job, but the isolation is already changing his perception of the rules. He's been shunted in here because nobody wants him around. On that basis, it isn't a job so much as a personal fiefdom. He can do whatever he likes.

He quickly finds the quality of the envelope is a good indicator of its contents. People who invest in decent envelopes tend to have something substantial to say. Even children's letters to Santa are always more precocious on expensive paper. Right now, Albert sits reading a child's demands for 'at least five hundred pounds in cash and another pony (and not black like that nag you sent last year)'.

'And merry Christmas to you too,' he says, as he rips the letter up.

Hearing footsteps, he tries to look busy.

A spotty eighteen-year-old enters with a small bundle of letters. He hands them to Albert in silence and then drifts away, everything about his manner suggesting not just a limited intellect, but the total absence of one.

Albert shuffles through the new mail as though it's his own. Some of the addresses are written in such an illegible scrawl they could be anything: ancient Sumerian, perhaps, or Egyptian hieroglyphs.

'And it's plausible, isn't it?' he says to himself. 'A letter going missing in the British postal system for five thousand years. I've heard of worse.'

And then he sees it.

A blank white envelope, not the best quality, granted, but respectable. And there, in the corner, a smiley face.

And, without another thought, he opens it.

17

Dear . . . I'm not going to call you the Universe, because I think that sounds daft. And I'm certainly not going to call you God. Croydon is the ultimate proof that God does not exist.

So let's just call you You. And I'll be Me.

Albert looks around guiltily. To break the rules by reading junk and drivel is one thing, but to find something like this . . .

He thinks of throwing the letter away, but he can't. Its words are already echoing in his head: '. . . let's just call you You. And I'll be Me.'

In as much as the letter isn't talking to anyone in particular, Albert already has the feeling it's talking to him. Surely that's sufficient justification for reading it.

He pulls his chair to the corner of the room, so that even if someone bursts in on him he'll still have time to hide the letter.

His heart beating faster now, he continues to read.

I feel like screaming. Not a good idea when you're sitting in an office full of people. Everyone's so drowsy with the post-lunch dip, I think one good scream would scare half of them to death. It would certainly finish off the woman next to me. So here I am, writing to you instead.

This is what I want to tell you: my life is a chocolate soufflé. The kind you spend hours making, then you pull it from the oven and it looks like a squashed cat. It's not dangerous. It's not a weapon of mass destruction. It's just not what it should be. It's a disappointment. You look at it and you think, Something went wrong. And that's the end of it, isn't it? You can't just pop it back in the oven and give it a few more minutes. It's not a mess on its way to becoming something else. It's just a mess.

I think my basic problem is I can't tell my family when they're making me unhappy. It sounds so simple, doesn't it? You feel sad, you speak out. But it just doesn't seem to work that way for me. I hear the words in my head and I feel them in my throat, but they don't actually come out. Instead, I get this overwhelming fear that my honesty will do something terrible to the other person, like it might accidentally lop off a couple of their limbs or strike them dead.

The other day I was trying to make conversation with my teenage daughter, asking about her studies, that kind of thing. And mid-sentence she tells me it would be better if I stopped asking because she's tired of having to explain the complex subjects to me, and tired of hearing me get the simple ones wrong. (Or maybe it was the other way round. I can't remember now.) What matters is, she said I only embarrass myself when I open my mouth. That I have, in fact, been embarrassing myself for many years and, for everyone's sake, it would be better if we put an end to it now.

What can you say to that? I, of course, basically said nothing, which is much like rolling onto my back and inviting her to kick me too. Which just makes me wonder, what the fuck is wrong with me?

Albert looks away, hopes that the F-word might some-how disappear if he just gives it a few seconds. He hates that word. It seems so needless.

I love the word 'fuck', don't you? Perhaps that's what I should have said to my daughter. 'What the FUCK?' That would have stunned her into silence. But I suspect that's another of my problems. In the absence of responding as I should, I worry I'm just storing up a massively inappropriate response for some later date.

I sometimes think it would be better if I really was a bit mad, because at least then people would realize they have to read between the lines of what I do and do not say. My daughter would insult me and immediately know that, although I seemingly caved in to her, what I really meant was 'Say that one more time and you'll be paying your own way through university'. Or I'd be talking to my husband and say something like, 'Let's get a dog' and he would know, in the context of my mental condition, what I really meant was 'I'm leaving you'. (You may like to know the dog died of old age a few years ago.)

I hadn't planned to tell you any of this, but it's surprisingly easy to confess things in a letter. It makes me think I should tell you about my teenage years too. How I looked for love in all the wrong places (on all fours, mostly). But perhaps that should wait for another time. Writing a letter seems like such a solid, old-fashioned thing to do, a little decorum is probably appropriate.

Does anyone even write letters any more? They feel like they belong to a different time, like milkmen, and getting film developed. Do you remember those days? Waiting a week to see if all your holiday snaps were crap and out of focus.

Albert stops reading. He hasn't had any photos developed for forty years, and somehow the thought makes him feel old, a relic from a different age.

The pictures were from a trip to Wales with his wife; their last holiday together, though they didn't know it at the time. When they got the photos back, most of them were pretty useless – much how Wales would look if they'd strapped themselves to a rocket and flown across it at low altitude – but they were memories nevertheless; reminders of something mad and silly that had made the holiday fun despite the rain. And after his wife died, they became a part of her legacy: the blurred pictures from when she'd been laughing too much to hold the camera steady; the nine different shots of Albert's feet when she'd accidentally pressed the shutter each time she'd stopped to kiss him.

It's strange how the years pass, isn't it? The way that some memories can seem so distant, like they never happened, and yet other things feel so real, you could almost reach out and touch them.

I've been thinking about the past a lot recently. About a special man in my past. But more about him next time.

Thank you for listening.

C.

18

THE TIN ISN'T meant for storing letters. The letter shouldn't even be in the house. Yet that's the thing about life: lots of things happen that shouldn't.

'It's like those kids that hang around on the street,' Albert explains to Gloria. 'You'd blush if you knew what they called old Mrs Hodgkins last week. It's true I've never liked the woman, but it doesn't seem right to even *say* that sort of thing, let alone shout it through the window of a moving bus.'

He hides the tin in the kitchen cupboard, still worried that the police may burst in at any moment looking for the one thing he never thought he'd have: a stolen letter.

'She was basically writing it to me.'

Gloria blinks once, twice, her mood hard to discern.

'She certainly didn't go to all that trouble just to have it burned by Royal Mail. No one in their right mind would write a letter just so it could burn.'

He pours Gloria a saucer of milk, a subconscious act of emotional blackmail.

'It's really just a case of finders, keepers, don't you think?'

Gloria purrs happily over her milk, which Albert naturally interprets as a sign of broader approval: that he is a good man with a good heart, incapable of committing a crime.

It's already early evening, time for Albert to begin his usual night-time ritual of cooking bland food and watching bland television, yet he paces the room, clearly in need of movement and activity. 'We could have mackerel for tea, couldn't we?'

Gloria looks up, her lips and whiskers spotted with milk.

'And some cake, perhaps. It's been a while since we've had a nice cake.' Before he's even considered the idea, he's pulling on his coat and heading for the door. 'I won't be long.'

Max isn't outside, but Albert is sure he'll hear the footsteps.

This'll confuse him, he thinks, as he strides past Max's potted plants. Going out at six o'clock!

He walks down to a small grocery store near his building, a battle-scarred place where a nervous shopkeeper peers out from behind a fortified till.

Browsing the aisles, Albert looks the same as ever: his face a little stiff, his eyes a tad too wide, much like a rabbit that's just been picked up by a predator. And yet, for the first time in years, something is stirring inside him. At first he thinks it's just indigestion again, but the sensation is more complex than that.

He puts two tins of mackerel into his basket and crosses to a shelf of cakes, his whole body feeling lighter than before.

He picks up a fruit cake with icing – a very indulgent treat for a Wednesday night – and realizes that if he allows himself to dream, if only for a second, then she will write more letters and he can think of her as a friend.

19

CAROL HAS ALWAYS thought of week-nights as the ultimate test of a family's health. At weekends, it's easy to forget you all hate each other – there are late nights full of alcohol and late mornings full of bed. But on a week-night, there's none of that protective cushioning, just the harsh reality of pleasure junkies in withdrawal.

On that basis, tonight should have been worse than usual. At least figuratively, Bob's testicular lump now looms over their lives, casting a deep shadow across everything. And still they've said nothing to Sophie, choosing instead to make Bob's illness another lie in a fundamentally dishonest marriage.

Yet tonight something has changed. Carol can't say what or why, she just feels happy.

It is, she decides, nothing to do with the letter. It's already been a couple of days since she posted it, and the initial catharsis of the confession quickly morphed into many emotions – excitement, fear, exhilaration, uncertainty

– before ultimately revealing itself to be a huge anticlimax. In terms of personal expression, it lacked visibility; less a message in a bottle than a broken bottle on the ocean floor.

From upstairs, Carol hears the telltale squeak of a floorboard. It's confirmation of what she already knows from the chill in the air: Sophie is alive. She's always marvelled at Sophie's ability to project her emotions, not just within a room, but even through walls and closed doors. And who knows the girl's range? Perhaps one day the entire population of London will figure out it's actually Sophie making them feel like crap. Carol can imagine them coming at night with pitchforks and burning torches.

'You want Sophie?' she'll say innocently. 'Of course, let me get her for you.'

As if on cue, Sophie enters the room, lithe and athletic. Assiduously avoiding Carol, she goes straight to Bob, who is sitting at the dining table engrossed in a jigsaw puzzle, though he isn't really doing the puzzle so much as staring at it, perplexed.

Sophie lingers over him for a few seconds, but there's only so long she can tolerate stupidity. She begins to finish it for him, her hands zigzagging across the table to find one piece—

'How did you do that?' he says.

Then another—

'Bloody hell!'

And another.

By now, Bob looks dumbfounded, as if he's always imagined the puzzle was supposed to be impossible; an elaborate exercise in disappointment and frustration.

Obviously wanting to gloat, Sophie glances at Carol, her smirk instantly becoming a frown. 'What are you so happy about?' she says.

'You know,' Carol replies, with a broad smile, 'I'm not even sure.'

'She's sitting in the same room as me, isn't she?' says Bob. 'That's enough to put a smile on any woman's face.'

Carol feels an urgent need to change the subject. 'Have you finished studying for the night?' She imagines this attempt at conversation earning her instant karmic rewards, the promise of a better and happier afterlife.

'I may pop out for a while,' says Sophie, in the general direction of Carol, more a radio broadcast than an actual response. Having fulfilled her side of the conversational deal, she turns back to Bob. 'Some money would help.'

'Tell me about it,' he replies, a playful tone in his voice. 'My wallet's in the kitchen, next to the chocolate cookies.'

'The empty packet of chocolate cookies,' adds Carol, still hopeful she can be a part of their banter.

Sophie doesn't even acknowledge the comment. As she heads for the kitchen, Bob calls after her, 'Are you going on a date or something?'

'No,' snaps Sophie, her inner Rottweiler always primed for attack. 'I'm just meeting friends for coffee.'

'We don't mind if you've met a nice boy,' adds Bob, clearly in the mood for mischief. 'It's okay to fall in love, you know. Twenty years from now you could be just like me and your mum.'

It's such a depressing thought that Carol isn't even

aware if the two of them continue talking. The notion of Sophie having the freedom to fall in love, her whole life still ahead of her, then throwing it away on a man like Bob, is so distracting, so overwhelming, she can only sit there in silence, merely pretending to smile now.

20

IT'S LIKE THE good old days again. Back when Albert was fresh out of the army and would tear around the streets of London on his brand-new postman's bicycle. Ever since getting the letter, he's gone to work early and stayed until he's certain that each day's post has been checked for undeliverable mail.

Today's haul is a paltry three envelopes, each of them on the kind of paper that makes him want to burn them straight away.

'Are you sure there's no more?' he says to his colleagues out in the sorting area.

'Albert, we've had over fifty thousand letters through here today. Do you want us to check them all by hand or what?'

He wants to say yes. He wants to volunteer for the job himself. He'll stay all night if he has to. It isn't as if he's slept properly the last few days anyway. That one letter has changed everything.

'And you're sure nothing's got lost in there?' He nods

towards the sorting machine. 'I mean, look at it. It's got secrets, that's plain to see.'

His colleagues stare back at him in muted disbelief. Watching them watching him, Albert realizes he may be losing his mind.

'Okay . . . Well, everything appears to be in order,' he says, as he begins to back from the room. He waves his three letters in the air and tries to appear genuinely pleased with them. 'These are . . . these are good additions to the collection. Thanks for your help.'

Word travels fast. Within minutes, Darren has popped in for 'a friendly chat'.

'So, how's it all going?' he says. His eyes seem to probe Albert, analysing him for signs of the dementia he's always suspected.

'Everything's shipshape,' replies Albert, but then worries that sounds too final. 'What I mean is, there's still lots to do, but I'm making good progress.'

'Right . . .' Darren glances around the room. 'And you're not finding it too . . . I don't know . . . isolated?'

'No, no, I'm enjoying it, actually. I mean, there's a job to be done, isn't there?'

'Er, yes.'

'And you wanted this to be my crowning triumph.'

'I suspect we're going to remember you for it, there's no doubt about that, but maybe for the rest of your time here you can just focus on organizing what we already have rather than worrying about the new stuff coming in.'

'But I want to keep on top of it all.'

Darren gives him a look of undiluted pity. 'Of course you do, but it'll be better for everyone if you just trust the guys to bring it to you, all right?' He gestures at the bulging sacks that line the room. 'You need to remember that all this stuff is useless, Albert. The truth is no one cares about it any more.'

21

LIKE PAP SMEARS and dental checks, Carol avoids seeing her mother whenever possible. Unlike pap smears and dental checks, Carol always comes away from her mother feeling mentally bruised and battered, swearing to herself it's the last time. And yet here she is, standing on the doorstep, preparing to start the cycle all over again. Even as she presses the bell she can't decide if it's guilt that brings her back or an admirable optimism, a deep-seated hope that this time everything will be different.

The door opens and there stands Deirdre, Carol's mother, her face devoid of emotion.

'I didn't hear the bell,' she says. 'Have you been here long?' Carol opens her mouth to respond, but Deirdre cuts across her. 'I dare say the batteries need replacing, but there's no point asking your father to do it, is there? It's just one more thing for me to do.'

She holds the door open and stands to one side, an unspoken invitation for Carol to enter.

For as long as Carol can remember, the house has had a pronounced atmosphere. Where other people's houses might feel studious, boisterous, even loving, this house simply feels silent. Not tranquil or meditative, but the silence of shameful secrets and slow decay – a silence so absolute, it's a physical sensation.

Carol enters the living room and immediately brightens. 'Hello, Dad.'

Her father moves his mouth in a lopsided yaw, but all that comes out is a jumbled noise; how 'hello' might sound if it was slowly played backwards.

Leaning on his wheelchair, Carol stoops to give him a kiss.

'He's been a handful all morning,' says Deirdre.

'Doing what? Breathing is about all he can do without you.'

'You don't understand because you don't live with it day after day.' She turns to her husband and raises her voice. 'Back in the old days, you'd have been drunk by now, wouldn't you? But not any more. We don't tolerate that sort of thing now, do we?'

Carol can feel the visit beginning its inexorable slide; can almost sense the wind in her hair as the day accelerates downhill. 'I don't think you need to keep mentioning the past,' she says.

'That's easy for you to say.' Deirdre bustles into the kitchen, her voice piercing the walls like heavy artillery. 'I just want him to remember that this house is run differently now.'

What she means is that God now lives among them. As

far as Carol is concerned, this says as much about God as anyone needs to know.

Her mother's official version of events is that the Good Lord rescued her from a tyrannical, drunken husband by striking him down with not just one stroke but three. By the time this divine hatchet job was complete, he was a shadow of his former self, entirely dependent on his wife for even the simplest pleasures.

If God is supposed to be all powerful, it seems odd to Carol that He didn't just give her father a change of heart – but, of course, that wouldn't have suited her mother at all: the God of her beliefs needs to be petty and vindictive, suburban in His morals and inclined to hold a grudge.

'How's Bob?' Deirdre calls from the kitchen.

'Oh . . . fine.' Carol decides now is not the time to be discussing cancer. Who knows what kind of spin her mother might put on news like that?

She looks at her father, immobile in the corner of the room. Moments like this used to be for their private jokes: making faces behind Deirdre's back; watching him take a quick swig from a well-hidden hip flask.

Her mother wasn't so vocal about her religious beliefs back then. They were just a hobby, the idle musings of a woman of limited intellect. It was the power vacuum left by her husband's strokes that changed everything, like weeds left to flourish when the gardener dies.

Deirdre returns with two mugs of tea. 'He's been knocking the phone off the hook again. I'm always thinking maybe you called and I missed it.'

'If that happened, I'd just call back later.'

Deirdre appears to ignore the comment. She glances at her husband. 'He manages to make everything ten times harder than it needs to be.'

'You should be pleased he can still manage to move at all.'

It's clear from Deirdre's facial expression that this comment is not appreciated. Perhaps it's a matter of faith, thinks Carol. If Deirdre really believes that it was God who smote her husband, the telephone is an awkward reminder that God isn't quite the man she thought.

For Carol, it's more interesting to ponder what's going through her father's mind on those rare occasions he lunges for the telephone. She can easily believe he's trying to call *her*, his silent lips always on the verge of screaming, 'Get me the fuck out of here!'

'I'm off to church this evening,' says Deirdre. 'You should join me. It's a sermon on the need for repentance in the Last Days.'

'No, thanks.'

Deirdre sighs. 'Your life's been too easy, that's the trouble. You've got your job, your house, a family of your own. You've never needed faith.' She eyes Carol for a moment, a vindictive tone creeping into her voice. 'I'd like to see you hit a few roadblocks in life, see how you cope then.'

Aware that her mother wants a confrontation – hers is a God of war, after all – Carol takes a deep breath and lets the comment pass. Although Deirdre can seem bossy and bullying, Carol tries to remind herself it's just the ideology talking: the woman beneath is small and frail, more like a child hiding inside a costume. For Deirdre, religion isn't an expression of faith so much as a surrogate personality, a lifelong guarantee that she'll never have to think or formulate her own opinions about anything. While some people try to calm their fears with drugs or alcohol, she's taken solace in dogma, a stark black-and-white world that offers all the insensibility of a crack pipe, but with an irritating smugness thrown in for free.

'And how's Sophie?'

'Fine. Busy with school.'

'It would be nice to see her some time.'

'She's seventeen. It's a difficult age.'

'As if you'd know anything about the difficulties of motherhood. You're lucky Sophie takes after Bob rather than you.'

Carol looks away, aware of the life draining from her world; a long-familiar sense of slowly dying in her mother's presence. She wants to get up and run, but all she can do is sit there and marinate in the toxicity.

The ringing of her mobile phone burns through the silence. Carol snatches it up on barely the second ring.

'Helen!'

'I was wondering if you're free for a cup of tea?'

Carol hesitates, aware that it's now or never. 'What?' she says in a shocked voice. 'Are you all right?'

'Carol? What are you talk—'

'I'll come over—'

'Carol—'

'No, no, don't be stupid! I'm with Mum and Dad right

now, but they'll understand. No, no, don't worry. I'll be there in . . . let's say thirty minutes.' She hangs up, looks grave. 'Helen's had an accident.'

'Is she all right?' says Deirdre.

'She slipped with a knife or something. There's a lot of blood.'

'Then surely she needs a doctor, not you.'

'No, no, the – the bleeding's stopped apparently, but she's a bit shaken up. And the kitchen is a nightmare, as you can imagine.' She almost jumps from her seat. 'But it was good seeing you. I'll give your regards to Bob and Sophie.'

She crosses the room and gives her father a peck on the cheek. "Bye, Dad.'

He gazes up at her with an imploring expression that could mean anything: panic, remorse, self-pity. So many emotions are appropriate, it's impossible to fathom his world any more.

'Does that mean you're actually coming over?' says Helen, as Carol retreats from her parents' neighbourhood.

'No, sorry.'

'Was it really that bad?'

'Oh, don't ask.'

'You could just try telling her the truth, you know.'

'What? "I hate you"? "I hate everything about you"? That wouldn't do much for our relationship, would it?'

'Strictly speaking, you don't have a relationship. And I know you don't want to hear it, but I'm not sure you can ever make things better with Sophie while you're still happy to wish your own mother dead.'

Carol doesn't reply, walks briskly now, wants only to crawl into a place of oblivion.

'So, are you going home?' says Helen, clearly wanting to steer their conversation back into safe territory.

'Home . . . Is that what it's called? Yes, I'm going home and I'm going to have a drink.'

'Define a drink,' replies Helen, anxiously. 'Are we talking about a glass of wine or three bottles of vodka?'

Carol doesn't want to make any promises she can't keep. 'Look, I've got to go.'

'Carol—'

'Don't worry, I'll be fine.'

22

ALBERT PEERS AT his reflection in the bathroom mirror. He isn't a vain man, but even he can see he isn't looking good. The sleepless nights and the constant anxiety have left him gaunt and pale.

'I don't even know her name!' he says to himself. 'I hardly know anything about her – except that she got around a bit as a teenager.' He hesitates over the memory. It feels a little strange to know that kind of thing before they've even established the basics. 'But people today, they're different like that.' And in his own way, he knows he's no better: they don't even qualify as acquaintances and he's already thinking about what to get her for Christmas.

He looks closer at his reflection. The hollowing cheeks. The dark circles beneath his eyes. And out of sight, deep inside, the worst thing of all: the knowledge that he's lonely. He's kept himself busy for decades denying that one fundamental truth, and now the deception has come crashing down because of a simple letter from a total stranger.

'Are you worried about retirement?'

This is probably the most compassionate thing Mickey Wong has ever said in his entire life, and it makes Albert feel even worse. That someone like Mickey can be reduced to pity is a sure sign that Albert has hit a new low.

'I've just had a lot on my mind,' says Albert. 'You know, with my cat and everything.'

Mickey nods understandingly and hands him that day's undeliverable mail. 'Because it's okay to be scared about retirement. It's a big change.'

'Thanks, Mickey. I appreciate it.' He pushes the stack of letters to one side, too depressed to risk the disappointment of checking them.

By now, Mickey is pacing the room with a philosophical air. 'I mean, when you think about it, retirement is a bit like sending a horse to the glue factory, isn't it? It's not actually the end, but the long-term prospects aren't good.' He clearly takes Albert's stunned expression as some kind of tacit agreement. 'So, really, it's no wonder you look a wreck. Your time's almost up, innit?'

He wanders away, his absence making the room feel even quieter than it did before.

In the long silence that follows, it occurs to Albert that the unwanted mail would make a perfect funeral pyre. When it's finally his time to move on to that bigger sorting office in the sky, what could be more fitting than to be carried there on the smoke of London's missing post? He doubts there are many places where you could discreetly burn a hundred thousand old letters and a dead body, but if it's possible anywhere it's South London. For most people on his estate, acrid smoke and the smell of charred flesh would probably be the least of their problems.

Then he sees it.

The edge of a face poking out from the bottom of that day's mail, but instead of a smile, this time it wears a scowl. Quite frankly the paper quality is disappointing too, but it's obviously from her.

Taking a seat in the corner of the room, Albert carefully opens the envelope.

As soon as he sees the letter, he knows something is wrong. The page is covered with a messy scrawl, as though she's written it on a fairground ride or during a particularly violent earthquake.

I have something to say!
   Fuck you! Yes, YOU!

Albert pauses, his heart pounding in his chest. He wants to stop reading, but it's too late.

I'm supposed to sit here and pour out my feelings. That's the idea, isn't it? Well, right now I feel like covering the page with ink and ramming it down your throat. Is that honest enough for you?

   Do you know what I think? If you really are reading this letter, it's only because you're a sad bastard. Your life is so empty, you need to listen to someone else's problems just to feel better about your own. That's the truth, isn't it? You're just some sad, lonely bastard.

You should be ashamed of yourself.

I'm never going to write again.

Do you hear me?

NEVER!

Albert slowly puts the letter down and sits in silence. Everything seems quieter now, not just the room but the world itself.

He tries to stand up, if only to put the letter in the bin, but he can't. His head is thick with a dazed, shell-shocked sensation, as though he's just survived a war, and not in the sense that the worst is over and everything will be okay now: instead, he feels like a man who has survived the horror of the trenches only to find his house is destroyed, all his children are dead, and his wife has just married the butcher.

'What do you mean "sick"?' says Darren. He looks concerned, probably more for his own sake than Albert's – how will he explain it to senior management if Albert drops dead on the job?

'I just need to take the afternoon off. Go and lie down.'

'Well, of course. And don't you worry about us, okay? We'll be fine without you.' He appears to regret the phrase. 'What I mean is, we'll miss you, but take as long as you need.'

'I'll be fine tomorrow.'

'No, really, I mean it. Take as long as you need.'

Fresh air helps, as does throwing away the letter, but Albert still feels as though he's labouring through the streets with a stab wound. He isn't doubled over in pain or dripping blood, but still he expects some reaction from passers-by – a scream, perhaps, or open-mouthed horror. But no: on the streets of South London, his dazed and damaged expression has found its natural habitat.

Part of him wants to throw away the other letter when he gets home, but he already knows he won't. If only for a brief moment, that letter was precious to him; he can't dismiss it now. If anything, it's a reminder of something innocent that has been lost, and what is his life, if not a mausoleum for memories like those?

He's still pondering the past when he steps from the lift and finds Max watering his plants.

If Max hadn't seen him, he would have gone quietly back downstairs and spent the next hour or two sitting in the park, but it's too late for that.

'What are you doing home at a time like this?' Max shouts.

Albert decides a dignified silence is the best response, but it only seems to make Max more aggressive.

'Come on, Albert, it's the middle of the afternoon. Either you're sick or you've been fired.' He studies Albert's face as he passes. 'You do look a bit peaky, but then you've always been the sickly sort. A bit of a weed, to be honest.'

Albert reaches his front door and fumbles with his keys.

'That cat of yours, he hasn't been skydiving again, has he?'

Albert tries to imagine how Max would sound falling six storeys onto bare concrete. It's a comforting thought.

'Look at you smiling to yourself, you fucking moron! That's why you're back early, isn't it?'

Still ignoring him, Albert steps inside his flat and closes the front door, but Max's voice remains clear.

'The Post Office has at long last realized you're the village idiot.'

True to his word, Albert is back at work the next morning. He hasn't slept well, but the same can be said for the whole week. At least last night his anguish had felt justified, even righteous.

Without the frenzied expectation of recent days, the morning passes more pleasantly. He can feel himself sinking back into a cocoon; isolated and alone but safe.

One of the trainees comes into the room with a letter.

'Just the one today,' he shouts, his every word thick with the smell of spearmint chewing gum.

Albert doesn't even bother looking at it, just tosses it towards one of the sacks. He misses, of course – he's never been very good at things like that. It's only as he goes to pick it up that he sees the smiley face on the envelope.

He stands over it, unsure if he even wants to know what the letter says.

And yet it's from her.

For him.

How can he not?

He picks it up and holds it, tries to weigh its merit, to gauge its intent.

Still nervous, he gently opens it.

Inside, a single sheet of paper, almost bare.

I'm SOOOOOO sorry. It was a bad day. I'll explain more next time.

xx

C.

PS. If it's any consolation, my hangover is so bad it feels like an act of divine vengeance.

23

CAROL DOESN'T KNOW if the letter was ever read, but that isn't the point. The world is already a bruising place to live without total strangers being mean to each other too.

She isn't ready to admit as much to Helen, but she's beginning to enjoy the process of writing letters. Even if they're just piling up in the corner of some dusty warehouse, it still feels like progress. Her angst has found a resting place and there's something soothing in that thought.

So soothing, in fact, that she now finds herself in a stationery store, its aisles packed full of paper for every occasion – colourful paper for the chronically cheerful, lined paper for people prone to dizzy spells, and gossamer airmail paper so delicate she can imagine it flying away even without the aid of an aeroplane.

She opens a pack of thick vellum paper and runs her fingers across its sheets. These are pages of substance in every sense. Her thoughts seem too mundane for paper like this, yet it's so beautiful that just touching it makes her happy.

She picks up a pack of matching envelopes and hurries to the cashier before she can change her mind. Tonight she's determined to write another letter and this time she knows exactly what she wants to say.

Bob's private specialist is great in as much as the office is posh and impressive, but the end result is that he still needs to lose a testicle.

'I don't quite believe it,' he says, as if he'd expected the price tag alone to miraculously cure him. 'They want to, you know, do it . . . this week.'

'And how do you feel about that?'

'I asked if they could just check it and then put it back.' He shakes his head, obviously still disheartened by the response. 'I suppose it's best just to take the bull by the horns . . .'

He doesn't sound very convinced, but his efforts to act like an adult are so endearing, so novel, Carol finds herself feeling proud of him anyway.

Before she even knows what's happening, Bob has reached for her hand. There's nothing sexual about it – he doesn't press her fingers against an erection as he's occasionally inclined to do – they just sit there smiling at one another.

Sophie enters the room with a plate of food and looks aghast at the two of them, evidently certain that this is the first stage of unstoppable foreplay.

'Don't mind me,' she says, turning on her heels.

'It's safe to come in,' calls Carol.

'No, it's okay,' replies Sophie, already out of sight. 'I'll watch TV in my room.'

Bob stares at the empty doorway as though Sophie is still there. 'We're lucky parents,' he says. 'I don't know what it was or how, but we definitely did something right.'

Deciding this is no time to spoil Bob's day with something so mundane as the truth, Carol simply smiles back at him. And in this unexpected moment of tenderness, it occurs to her that the lie of their married life knows no bounds; that even in the absence of love and respect, here they are, the picture of domestic harmony, to all appearances like any of the other happily married couples to be found at this exact moment across London.

24

HER NAME IS Connie. That's the right sort of name for a troubled young lady, the kind who's been a bit of a tart in her time, but who has a good heart underneath it all.

She could be a Christine, of course, but Albert hopes not. Christine sounds like an arch, manipulative young woman. There'd be no reforming a wayward Christine. And she can't be a Carol or a Cynthia because girls called Carol and Cynthia are just too ordinary for that.

'I don't mean that in a bad way,' he says to Gloria. 'There was a time when decent men wanted nothing more than a plain, ordinary girl. Being average was something a woman could really aspire to.'

Gloria blinks at him, reserving her judgement as ever.

'Girls like that are all that's left of a decent world. You certainly wouldn't find a girl called Cynthia on all fours with a stranger.'

So her name is definitely Connie and her letters to Albert will help her find peace, so that eventually they'll meet. He'll probably end up being a bit of a father to her, he already knows that. Though not too much of a father. He can't put her over his knee, for instance, even though he suspects it would do her some good. He'll have to be more of a father in the church-going sense, but without all the baggage of Heaven and Hell.

In front of him, the television flickers in its usual night-time routine, but this time the sound is off. Albert wishes he'd tried it like this years ago. Now he can at least kid himself that the programmes are saying something intelligent and interesting. He actually finds it quite pleasant to sit and wonder if he's missing something worthwhile, rather than experiencing the disappointment of turning up the sound and realizing he's not.

He glances back at Gloria, her eyes flickering in the light of a soap-powder commercial.

'I just need to be strong, that's all. I've let myself down this last week. Let myself down and let Connie down too.' They watch together as another advert comes on. A woman in a white lab coat is pouring large beakers of fluid over sanitary towels, though with the sound off it's hard to tell what the point is. Regardless, the young woman at the end of the ad looks happy.

'What rubbish. She wouldn't be running for the bus like that, not with half a pint of water in her knickers. It's enough to give someone a rash, even at her age.'

Somehow the thought sends his mind spinning back to Connie.

'She needs a strong man in her life. I think that's obvious.'

He glances at Gloria for her agreement, but she sits with her eyes closed now, clearly bored by the television and his monologue.

Without thinking, he lowers his voice. 'I know I'm not the ideal man for the job, but all things are relative, aren't they? I mean, for a girl like Connie, I'd be more than good enough. Compared to the things she's done in her life, I'm practically Clark Gable.'

25

Don't worry, I'm not going to scream at you. I was a bit crazy last time (very drunk, actually). Sorry about that. I'd been to see my parents. If you were familiar with my mother you wouldn't need me to say anything else. She's the kind of woman who could drive a saint to whisky and violence. My father used to be a stabilizing influence, which is ironic considering he was an alcoholic, but now he's paralysed and everything is just one big clusterfuck. (I think that word is appropriate here.)

I tell myself it's okay to just avoid her, but then guilt sets in and I begin thinking maybe it'll be better next time. Famous last words.

It doesn't help that I feel like it's my fault my mother has the personality of a toxic-waste dump, and that my father is a vegetable in a wheelchair. With that much guilt to carry, it's a miracle I kept myself to vodka the other night – though that probably says more about my local supermarket than me. I mean, maybe if it sold heroin and crystal meth, the evening would have worked out differently. (As you can imagine, it feels great to be saying that at the age of thirty-eight. I've made such a success of my life!)

You know what? I feel like I should give you a name. I mean, I've gone to all the trouble of buying fancy paper (I hope you're impressed), it seems a shame not to address it to someone.

This is a bit like being a parent all over again, trying to figure out a name that won't get your kid beaten up or hated for the rest of its life. I don't think my own parents scored too highly on that, by the way. I mean, they called me (and I know I'm not supposed to be using names, but what the hell, the whole point of these letters is to live dangerously, right?) . . . so, drum roll, please . . . they called me Carol! I mean, Carol! If it's not an irritating song being played on an endless loop then it's, I don't know, it sounds a bit like a brand of toilet roll to me. Or something from one of those health-food shops. 'Just take a spoonful of Carol between meals and it flushes the bowels right out.'

So, back to you. I think you should have a solid sort of name, like Edward or Charles. Though actually I don't like either of those, sorry. Robert, of course, is a relatively solid name, but for personal reasons we won't be using that. I like Toby. Harry's nice too. But before you start thinking I like names ending in y, I think Jimmy is a terrible name. It sounds like a cheap brand of oven cleaner, the kind that doesn't actually work. Anyway, all those y names are a bit too chummy for this, don't you think? Toby and Harry are probably great to meet up with for a pint, but I don't think they're the kind you'd want to entrust with your darkest secrets. I'm no Catholic, but I wouldn't feel comfortable confessing to someone called Harry. Maybe it's just me.

I want to call you Richard. I want to write this to Richard. But you're not Richard, I know that.

That name. Carol stops writing, can feel her heart pounding in her chest.

The house is silent, Bob and Sophie both fast asleep. And here she is, writing a letter that will never be read.

'Better if it isn't ever read,' she mutters to herself. The things she wants to say tonight, it will be enough just to put them on paper, to finally acknowledge them and let them go.

It seems fitting to be doing this while Bob and Sophie sleep. There's a purity to it: they're here in the house, close to her, and yet entirely removed. It's as if this one moment has brought the truth of their lives into sharp focus.

Dear Richard

I resent Sophie. And I blame you. Well, that's not true. I blame myself for loving you. But I blame you for being so easy to love.

It's not that I hate Sophie. I mean, hate is a bit strong, isn't it? I'll save that for when she's older.

Just kidding! I don't think parents are entitled to hate their children. I don't think we have the right to, for any reason (and yet here I am, quite happy to admit I don't like her much. It's probably all the same in the end, don't you think?).

I suppose I resent her for the decisions I've made. The things I've done, and not done, for the sake of motherhood. I know I shouldn't blame her for my decision to marry Bob, but it's hard not to when she's really the only reason I went through with it.

In her defence, I wanted to believe I was in love. Not that I had any understanding of what love was back then. I mean, it's easy to fall in love if your only definition of intimacy is that the guy hangs around for a while after he comes. When I look back now, it seems like I didn't really fall in love at all. I just gave up hope.

It's not that Bob's a bad man. He's not. In fact, he's probably perfect for someone. (I'm not sure I ever want to meet that kind of woman, but I wish them all the best.) And you know what? I think they could be very happy together. Genuinely happy, rather than this fake happiness I've sold him. He believes it's real, but that doesn't make it any better, does it?

And all these years I've tried to tell myself it was a noble act, staying with him for the sake of his child. And now . . . now the only thing I know for certain is that I don't have the opportunity to do it all again. Even when I leave him (note the 'when', not 'if'), I don't get those years back.

'Carol?' Bob wanders into the room in his pyjamas, his eyes squinting in the light, his hair a tangled bed-head. 'What are you doing?'

Startled, Carol quickly turns the light off, plunging the whole room into darkness.

'What the—'

'You shouldn't be in bright light. You'll never get back to sleep.'

'But I can't even see you now.'

'You don't need to.'

Bob groans, his voice thick with sleep. 'Why are you up?'

'I'm writing a letter.'

'But you don't write letters. Nobody writes letters any more.'

'It's to an old friend. From the office.'

'Can't you send an email?'

'No, she's, er . . . on a farm now. In Australia. A sheep farm. They only have radio.' She struggles for something else to say. 'I've just found out she's pregnant.'

'What – at three o'clock in the morning?'

'No, I mean I found out today . . . yesterday. And then I couldn't sleep. Did I wake you up?'

'By writing downstairs in silence, you mean? No . . .' He yawns. 'The bed just felt empty without you.'

'You should go back to sleep. I'll be up in a while.'

'Come now.'

'There's no point. I can't sleep.'

'But you can't write a letter in the dark.'

'I'm going to turn the light back on.'

'Then it's no wonder you can't sleep.'

Deciding a quick cuddle may do the trick, she tries moving towards him, but doesn't see a dining chair in the way.

'Ow, fuck!' she yells, as her shin slams into it.

'What happened?'

'No, no, I'm fine.' Her leg begins to throb. 'It's nothing.'

From upstairs, the sound of movement. Sophie turning in her sleep.

As silence descends once more, Carol reaches out into the darkness and slides her hands around Bob's fleshy mid-section. 'Look, just go to bed, okay? I'll be up in a little while.'

'You promise?'

'Of course.' She kisses him on the forehead, his scruffy hair tickling her nose. 'Just go to sleep.'

She listens as he shuffles away, the sound slowly fading into the subtle squeak of an upstairs floorboard.

When she turns the light back on, it seems too bright, too harsh for this time of night. Shielding her eyes from the glare, she goes back to the letter.

What am I trying to say? Even I've lost track. This is what happens to a woman when she doesn't have enough friends. There's Helen, bless her, but she's changed a lot since you were around. Divorce and single motherhood seem to have whittled her down to something too fragile for everyday life. She's still my best friend, but I need a *yin* to balance her *yang*, if you know what I mean. I'd certainly like a friend with better taste in tea.

Anyway, before I lose my mind and begin wandering the streets of Croydon drooling on myself, I just want to say this: I take responsibility for the decisions I've made, even the really bad ones. It was my decision to stay with Bob. My decision to try and think of Sophie's needs rather than my own. Maybe I've used that as an excuse to avoid doing the things that scare me, I don't know. It doesn't matter any more, does it?

I used to think I was acting with some kind of integrity; that by staying with Bob I was investing in my future relationship with Sophie. I can see now that parenthood doesn't really work like that. Happiness is all you can give a child; everything else is just decoration. And if you can't be happy by example, you can't give them any kind of happiness at all.

So it was all a bit of a fuck-up, wasn't it? I would have been better off dumping Bob and moving in with you. But that's something I could only know with fifteen years of hindsight. And now you're gone and it's all too late.

I'd love to know what you'd think of Sophie. I suspect I'm the only person who wants her to be different. I mean, she's smart, and she's friendly with everyone but me. I'd just like to see her be a bit more 'young', I suppose. To forget about being the over-achiever just for a little while, and have some fun. I've got this horrible feeling that if she doesn't get teenage craziness out of her system now, it will only come for her later in life. I don't want to see her getting to her mid-thirties trying to figure out where it all went wrong. Then everything really would have been a waste.

Time for bed.

xxx

Carol

She stares at the letter, her first real communion with Richard in years. If she knew how to reach him, she'd send it in a heartbeat, would go out right now to walk the darkened streets if necessary.

She doesn't know where he is, yet the simple act of writing to him has made the memories burn brighter; has made him feel close again.

She wonders if this is the power of belief: that something can be irrational, mad and ill-advised, and yet for a brief moment it makes all things seem possible.

Overcome by the thought, she picks up her pen again.

PS I know you're never going to see this, Richard, but if there's any chance at all, please get in touch.

She lingers over the words, dreams of him somehow reading them.

To hear his voice again. To touch his face. To have a second chance.

Carried on that wave of emotion, she kisses the page and seals it in an envelope.

26

IT'S A FREE medical, but Albert really can't see the point. He's getting old. Things are beginning to wear out. He doesn't need a doctor to tell him that. Nor does he care what his cholesterol is, or his blood pressure. He's managed to live sixty-five years without knowing any of these things, so why start now?

'I'm just going to take a blood sample,' says the doctor. 'You might feel a little prick, but that's all.'

He stabs the syringe into Albert's arm.

'Ow!'

'Sorry. Taking blood has never been my strength.' He attaches a large tube to the needle and watches while it starts to fill with blood.

'Am I supposed to fill that right up?' says Albert. It looks an awful lot of blood just for a simple test.

'Oh, why not? It seems a shame to do things by halves.'

'I'm not sure I have that much to spare.'

'Well, if you begin to feel dizzy and black out, then no,

you don't.' He smiles at his own joke. 'But I dare say you'll be fine.' He taps at the tube. 'If you squeeze your hand into a fist like this . . . yes, that's right . . . and then pump it like so . . .'

Albert watches as the blood pulses into the tube, a rhythm of crimson spurts.

'I normally have a nurse for this sort of thing,' says the doctor, 'but she's off sick.'

Albert is unsure how he's supposed to respond. 'Physician, heal thyself' comes to mind, but the doctor has probably heard that a hundred times before. He decides on something more supportive. 'There's a bad cold doing the rounds,' he says. 'Some of the people at work have had it.'

'Oh, it's not a cold. She's got syphilis.' For the first time this morning, he actually sounds pleased. 'I've never seen a case of syphilis before, so it's really been quite satisfying.'

Evidently happy with the blood sample, he yanks the tube from Albert's arm, then fumbles about while Albert continues bleeding on himself.

'Here you go.' He liberally douses Albert's arm with antiseptic. 'It might sting a little.'

'Only a bit,' replies Albert, through gritted teeth.

The doctor hands him a small piece of cotton wool. 'Just press this against your arm for five or ten minutes and you'll be fine.'

He retreats behind his desk, looks relieved to at last get some distance from Albert.

'So,' he says, 'you'll be retiring soon?'

'This month.'

'And you're aware that the mortality rate for men of your age climbs steeply in the first year or two after retirement?' He says it with a hopeful tone, as if early death is one of the few things that makes his job interesting. 'We see a lot of cancer, strokes, heart attacks, that sort of thing.'

'I think I'm in relatively good shape.'

Albert waits for the doctor to agree with him, but he's too busy checking his notes.

'I was a little concerned by your lungs,' he says. 'Do you smoke?'

'No.'

'Have you ever had tuberculosis?'

'No. Is there something wrong?'

'Not really. I mean, nothing that showed up on the X-ray, which is just as well because that always captures the *really* deadly stuff.' He says it with unashamed relish. 'In your case, though, things appear to be fine. It's just when I used the stethoscope, your lungs sounded – how shall I say? Fragile. My advice is to be careful with them, give them a rest from time to time.'

'My lungs?'

'Yes.'

Albert wonders how he's supposed to do that. Perhaps take them out occasionally, give them a rinse. They've already established he isn't a smoker, so it's difficult to know what else he can do besides breathing less.

'There is just one more test I need to do.' The doctor pulls on a pair of latex gloves and carefully applies lubricant to the tip of his index finger. 'When did you last have your prostate checked?'

'That depends,' says Albert, with a rising sense of panic. 'Where is it?'

Since it was his first real medical in almost fifty years, Albert comforts himself it will also be his last. He can live the rest of his days in peace, knowing that nobody else will do what has just been done.

It's enough to make him pale, knowing that twenty minutes earlier he'd been bent over a desk and probed. He's heard about people who do that kind of thing for pleasure – and a lot more besides, if the tabloids are anything to go by – but he's never imagined it happening in the name of healthcare too. The NHS will be using gerbils next, and latex toys.

He wants to go back to work and see if there's a letter from Connie, but as usual Darren has told him to take the rest of the day off.

Having just been fingered by another man, it occurs to him he should really go and sit in a church for a while – though he didn't actually enjoy the experience, so a long hot bath will probably suffice.

Even while Albert is still in the lift, he can sense Max will be outside tending his plants; the proverbial canary in the cage, he can feel the way Max's personality fills the air, like a cloud of toxic gas.

Sure enough, as the lift doors open, there he is. And this time not alone, but accompanied by his wife.

Max's wife is rather like Kim Jong-il, in the sense that she's almost never seen in public, and when she is, it's always with a sickly demeanour and a bad perm.

On this occasion, she's standing in the front door perfectly still, so that from a distance she actually looks dead – a stiff corpse gently basking in the sunlight of a winter afternoon.

'You part-timer,' shouts Max, as Albert approaches. 'Do you even do any work any more?'

Albert wants to say he's had a medical, but Max has crafty powers of deduction. It's best to avoid the subject.

'I had some personal business to attend to.'

'Oh, I see,' says Max, in a mock-posh voice. 'Not the Queen's business on this occasion, but one's own.'

Thinking Max's wife might appreciate knowing that other people hate her husband, Albert gives her a sympathetic smile.

'What are you looking at?' she says, in a frail, breathless voice.

It's obvious she can't move her neck very easily, but her eyes follow him as he passes. Inevitably her pupils reach their full extent and Albert moves out of range. By the time she's finished turning her head in his direction, he's already unlocking the front door.

She opens her mouth to speak, but nothing comes out.

She tries again.

'Fucking dickhead!' she gasps.

'Yeah, you tell him,' says Max. He turns to Albert and raises his voice. 'If I had grandkids, I'd keep them away from you.'

'But I like kids,' says Albert, genuinely hurt.

'See?' says Max, to his wife. 'The man's a pervert.'

The rest of the evening passes in the usual way. There's silent television to fill the darkness, and idle chit-chat with Gloria. As the evening wears on, however, Albert finds himself coming back to the doctor's warning that he has fragile lungs.

'I've never heard such rubbish,' he says, but even mentioning it seems to make the prognosis more threatening.

He clears his throat, wondering now if it's the start of a cough. 'Anyone would think I'm going mad.'

Yet as soon as he's said the words, he starts to wonder if this, too, might be true.

27

Carol doesn't regret posting her name to the great unknown. It's an act of optimism, the kind of unexpected craziness that makes her feel more alive. The worst that can happen is she'll get found out by a confused and embarrassed postman – and she can always deny everything. At the very least it will confirm her letters are being read.

For the first day or two there's a faint rush, but then the hopes and fears begin to fade. The more she thinks about it, the more it seems that writing letters really is a religion – a futile practice that offers comfort only for as long as one keeps up the pretence.

Fortunately there's Bob's lumpy testicle to fill the void. The long-awaited operation takes place at the end of the week and demands that Carol once again play the role of attentive wife.

When she arrives at the hospital, she finds it has a discreet, low-key appearance at odds with its true nature. Inside, men and women are fighting disease, being cut open, presumably even dying, but from outside it could almost be a hotel. Sitting in the car park, she can't shake off the thought that at any moment someone might wander out with a piña colada and an inflatable sun-lounger.

Even after she enters the building, the experience remains surreal. She hasn't even reached the reception desk when a nurse approaches, her manner more akin to a concierge or a well-fed slave. 'Mrs Cooper?' she says, with a warm smile.

Carol wonders how she can tell. Is Bob the only patient today, or does Carol just look like the kind of woman who'd be married to a man like him?

'Your husband is quite comfortable,' the nurse continues. 'Everything went very well.'

He only had a bollock removed, thinks Carol. He could have done it himself with a Stanley knife and an Elastoplast.

'. . . he was sedated for the operation,' the nurse is explaining, 'but that's wearing off now.'

She leads the way through quiet, empty corridors.

'Where's everyone else?' says Carol.

'We like to keep this a very boutique experience.'

Carol decides this is a polite way of saying all the other patients have died in botched procedures. Maybe this is why the nurse is so pleased that Bob survived. 'They normally die like flies,' she can imagine the nurse saying. 'But at least we have fresh flowers in all the public areas.'

The nurse stops. 'You might find him a bit sleepy, but other than that he's back to normal.'

She gently opens a door and ushers her inside, closing it so quietly Carol doesn't even know she's gone.

In front of her, Bob sleeps peacefully. He looks smaller than before, as if something bigger than a testicle is missing, and Carol finds herself pondering the irony that less of him makes her like him more.

She takes a seat beside him just as he opens his eyes.

'Hello, sleepy.'

'Oh, hello. Have you been here long?'

'Just arrived.' She struggles for something to say. 'Fancy a blow-job?'

'Now you offer.'

'And it's only available today, I'm afraid.'

'I can't even think about my nuts without them hurting. Without it hurting, I mean.'

'I'll take that as a no.'

'You can order a drink if you like. They've got a wine list, would you believe it?'

'No wonder you're feeling tired. That can be the official story, can't it? You wandered into this posh place thinking it was a bar. Next thing you know, you wake up in bed with a testicle missing.'

Bob doesn't smile. 'Believe it or not, Carol, I wasn't planning to tell everyone. Have you told Helen?'

She hesitates. 'Only that you're not feeling well.'

Bob doesn't look convinced.

'This is Helen, the overwrought mother of Jane, we're talking about. She's got enough of her own problems.' She says it with total confidence, certain that even passers-by and the congenitally blind can tell Helen is a woman burdened by life.

Bob obviously agrees. 'Sorry,' he says. 'I probably sound like a right prick.'

'Don't worry,' she replies, with a disarming smile. 'I'm used to it by now.'

Even at the best of times, there's a tense atmosphere at Carol's house. Tonight, with Bob away, it actually feels baited, as if Sophie has rigged the entire building with tripwires and limpet mines.

'I don't even know why she's here,' says Carol, on the phone to Helen. 'As far as she's aware, Bob's away on business. If I was her, I would have stayed out the whole night.'

'And ended up having sex with some random stranger.'

'Helen!'

'But it's true, isn't it? You weren't exactly a saint at her age. I think you should count yourself lucky she has her head screwed on.'

'So tightly it's stuck.'

'Carol, your teenage daughter is at home on a week-night studying—'

'I didn't say she's studying, I just said she's being quiet. When I was her age, that would have meant I was dead, but with Sophie . . . Is it something to do with intellect, do you think, this need for silence?'

'I don't think it can be a bad thing.'

'Really? Can a person not practise Satanism in silence? For all I know she's up there trying to raise Pan. Or maybe she's on her webcam showing her tits to some bloke in Belgium.'

'You could always go and check on her. It might help break the ice.'

'Helen, when you break ice, you fall into water. Even if you don't drown, you die of hypothermia.'

'That's not a very optimistic view of motherhood.'

'And what? You're going to give me tips? Let's face it, one of the reasons we're such good friends is that we're both crap at this.' There's a long silence at the other end of the line. 'Sorry, that didn't come out quite the way I had in mind.'

'What – it was supposed to be witty banter? "Helen, you're a crap mother and your daughter hates you."'

'I didn't say that.'

'But it's true, isn't it? She does.'

Carol wants to say something comforting about it all getting better in time, but she knows that probably isn't true.

'At least you're sounding more cheerful,' says Helen. 'Have you written a letter like I suggested?'

'No.' Carol can hear the defensive, guilty tone in her voice, but Helen seems oblivious.

'Well, there's a definite change in you. I can sense it.'

'Maybe I'm just beginning to believe the end is in sight with Bob.'

'So you still think it's over?'

'You thought one less testicle might make all the difference to our relationship?'

'You know what I mean.'

'Well, he's home tomorrow. Then we find out what's going on with the lump.'

'And if it's serious?'

'Said the eternal optimist.'

'I'm just being realistic. I presume most doctors aren't in the habit of ripping out testicles just for the sake of it.'

Carol hesitates over her response, can already feel herself on a flight to Athens – can feel the thrust of the engines as the plane accelerates down the runway, as it lifts from the ground and carries her up through clouds to a place of eternal sunshine.

'No,' she says, 'he'll be fine.'

28

THE DAY AFTER his medical, Albert is back at work, and just in time to receive Carol's letter.

It arrives at the sorting office not long after Albert himself, its contents waiting to brighten his day, not just with words, but with a name and a telephone number, too.

He has no awareness of its proximity as he goes about his morning; no sense of its progression through a system that will inevitably bring it to his desk.

It's only when Darren enters the room that the day becomes something other than ordinary.

'We're having a clear-out,' he says. 'It's time to get rid of everything old.' Albert looks alarmed and even Darren appears to reconsider his words. 'The old letters, I mean.' He points at five sacks leaning against the far wall. 'Have you checked these ones? Can they go?'

'Yes, that lot can all be chucked.'

'Albert, we're not in the habit of "chucking" mail. We're

disposing of it. In an ethically, environmentally and fiscally responsible manner.'

'What does that mean exactly?'

'We're selling it to a recycling facility. It's going to be pulped and made into, I don't know, loo roll and beer mats or something.' He watches as two trainees begin to haul sacks from the room. 'That's it, lads, chop-chop.'

For a second he looks exhilarated, an emperor with minions at his bidding.

'And what should I be doing?' says Albert.

'What you always do, Albert. Just . . . just keep up the good work.' He turns and follows the trainees out, the dusty air spinning curlicues in his wake.

'"Do what you always do,"' says Albert. 'Well, in that case I might make myself a cup of tea.'

While he's gone, the day's new mail arrives, the creamy envelope of Carol's letter tucked in among the pile.

Unfortunately, without him around, it falls to one of the trainees to take charge of the situation.

'Stick it in here,' he says, holding a sack open. 'This lot's all going.'

Even if Albert were to come back now, he might still see the letter, its smiley face peering out from the shadows.

In his absence, however, the young man ties the sack shut and drags it away, removing Carol's letter from this world while Albert blithely waits for his tea to steep.

29

BRINGING BOB HOME is really just the warm-up act. The highlight of the day, for better or for worse, is the telephone call expected later that afternoon from his specialist. In some backroom laboratory, Bob's stray testicle has been sliced up like Serrano ham and is now yielding its secrets. Soon everyone will know the truth.

Bob tries to put a brave face on the wait. 'We might go to the pub tonight. What do you think?'

'I think a quiet night would be better, Bob.'

'But we'll be celebrating!' There's a desperate quality to his voice, a fear in his eyes that pleads for Carol to play along.

'Actually, why not?' she says. 'A night at the pub could be nice.'

'Might be good to invite Tony and Mandy too. What do you think?'

'Of course, more the merrier!'

Bob decides to phone them, his hands trembling as he waits.

'Tony!' he shouts, in a bullish voice straight from a stage performance. 'Yeah, all right, mate, all right. Look, we were thinking of a night down the pub . . .' Carol realizes that even his body language has changed, that he now has the wired, wide-eyed quality of a child who's drunk too much orange squash. 'No way! Well, that's an amazing offer! Yeah, we'd love to!'

An amazing offer. Carol feels her heart sink. When it comes to people like these, no offer can be good.

'Yeah, we'll come round at seven! Great!'

He hangs up and visibly shrinks, all his fears and concerns rushing back. 'They've invited us over,' he says, as he returns to the sofa and sinks into the cushions. 'Tony thought we could have a barbecue. A sort of end-of-summer thing.'

'It's almost November.'

'But it's quite mild. For the time of year, anyway.'

'Relative to it being winter, you mean?'

'It's British optimism, isn't it?' He's clearly encouraged by Tony's patriotic urge to stand outside on a cold, damp night and eat badly cooked food. 'Maybe Sophie can join us too.'

'She's at hockey practice. Anyway, she'd rather drink weed-killer than be with the four of us.'

'But it could be a nice evening.'

With that, the telephone begins to ring and all thoughts of evenings, nice or otherwise, vanish.

30

ALBERT HAS ALWAYS imagined that getting his bus pass would be a celebratory occasion. Over the years, he's heard of people hankering for this moment, as though the whole point of life is to grow old and get free bus travel. Yet today, the day his bus pass arrives, he feels only a sinking sensation.

It doesn't help that he still hasn't heard from Connie. In the absence of a letter from her, everything seems greyer and less satisfying than it should. Worse, the bus pass feels like a reminder that he's now one of the elderly; that even before he's officially retired, he's become one of that aimless group of people who have so little to do they're given free bus travel as a way of occupying themselves. He's seen their faces peering out of bus windows over the years, people who've spent all day going round in circles – maybe as a way of keeping warm and dry, or maybe they just can't remember where they live; it's all the same in the end.

Even the timing seems like a cruel joke. *Now you're getting too old to enjoy it, here's a bus pass! Now you're about to become frail and housebound, here's unlimited travel!* So much for government largess.

Yes, it's nice to know he can get on a bus – any bus! – and go somewhere new, but it's taken him years to figure out the movements of the thugs in his own neighbourhood; it seems reckless to just wander off somewhere totally unfamiliar. He'd be picked off in seconds.

Maybe that's the point, he decides. It isn't really a free bus pass at all, it's a way of keeping numbers down. By weeding out the pensioners who are still active and mobile, the government is left only with the weak, and one decent cold spell will be enough to finish them off.

Too self-conscious to use the pass this morning, Albert waits for his journey home to give it a try, and even then he lets all the other passengers get on first. Part of him expects the driver to take one look and kick him off. '*You?* A pensioner? Get out of here, you cheeky bugger!'

But, no, the driver doesn't even look at the pass. His eyes are half shut, heavy with sleep, and there's a conspicuous damp patch on his shirt breast.

'Is that it, then?' says Albert.

'Is what it?' snarls the driver.

Albert holds up his pass again. 'It's just I'm new to all this – I only got it today.'

'And, what, you want me to sing you happy birthday or something?' He pulls away from the kerb with such a jolt that Albert is sent stumbling down the aisle.

As he clambers into one of the few empty seats, he

realizes he is surrounded by the elderly, less a bus than a mobile ghetto.

'You should always try to sit down before it starts moving,' says the old lady next to him. She has a gentle voice and kindly eyes. From beneath a headscarf, wispy white hair flutters in an imperceptible breeze. 'This one thinks he's a rally driver, that's the problem.'

'I normally sit upstairs,' replies Albert.

'Are you mad? That's where the ruffians go. I've seen them. I've even heard them sometimes, stomping about up there and shouting . . .' Her words trail off into silence and for a moment Albert thinks she's lost her train of thought. Just as suddenly, she speaks again: 'If I was the driver, do you know what I'd do? I'd find a nice low bridge and *accelerate*.' She thumps the palm of her hand to add more emphasis to the carnage she has in mind. 'That would teach them a thing or two.'

Like not letting crazy old women drive buses, thinks Albert. He smiles at her. 'Well, if ever I see you behind the wheel of a bus, I'll remember not to sit upstairs.'

'Good, because I won't be giving any warnings. Surprise is the key to a successful attack.' She nods happily. 'I'd bomb their homes if I could.'

Albert turns and looks for a seat elsewhere.

'I think I might move to the back,' he says, hoping not to offend her. 'The, er, the vibration of the engine is, um, good for my rheumatism.'

The woman looks intrigued, obviously intending to share this tip with others. Before she can ply Albert with any questions, he's shuffling off down the aisle, gripping the seats for support as the bus weaves at speed through the streets of South London.

When he reaches the back, the roar and heat of the engine make it feel more like a factory floor than public transport. Albert nods at his new companions, two men and a woman. 'I like it better back here.'

'There's no need to be polite,' replies one of the men. 'Everyone knows she's mad.'

'Just don't get her started on young people,' adds the woman.

'"I'd bomb their homes if I could,"' says the other man.

They all start laughing, and even Albert finds himself chuckling now, swept up by the easy, unexpected camaraderie of strangers on a bus.

31

BOB STARTS THE telephone call standing up, but sits down after the first ten seconds.

'Okay,' he mumbles, at the end of the conversation, 'thanks for calling.'

As he gently puts the receiver back in its cradle, Carol doesn't need to ask what the specialist said. Everything about Bob appears overwhelmed, as though even simple motor functions are becoming too much effort. Finally, he gives in to gravity and crumples into the chair. 'Oh, God . . .'

'We'll get through this, Bob.' She puts her arms around him, feeling more protective of him now than she has in years. 'We'll beat this.'

'I can't go to the barbecue.'

'Of course we're not going.'

'No, you have to go.'

'What?'

'They'll think something's wrong if we don't turn up.'

'Of course something's wrong!'

Bob starts to cry.

'Sorry,' she says, 'that's not—'

'I don't want to die.'

'You're not going to die.'

'How do you know?' he gasps, through his tears.

'Because . . . because I believe in hope.' She's aware of the irony. Hope – the thing that promises her freedom from him – is now the very thing tying her down. She squeezes him tighter, certain of her words despite the price she'll have to pay. 'I know we're going to beat this because I'm here to fight it with you. And I'm an evil cow when I'm pissed.'

'What a shame Bob couldn't come,' says Tony, as he slathers a rack of baby ribs with something sticky and heavily processed. 'The sickly wanker!'

'I think it was something he ate at lunchtime,' says Carol. 'He just needs to rest.'

'Something he ate at lunchtime! How about a dirty minge with a bad case of the clap? And I don't mean you, love.' He chuckles to himself, clearly unconcerned that he's talking to the man's wife.

'No,' says Carol, 'I'm pretty sure he wasn't doing that today.'

'Then there's his problem! I reckon a bit of promiscuity does wonders for the immune system. What do you think, Mandy?'

'What's that, Tone?' She jiggles into view with a plastic beaker of vodka and an absent look that suggests she's been drinking for some time.

'Fucking around,' shouts Tony, without a hint of embarrassment. 'Fucking around kills germs!'

Mandy appears to give it serious consideration. 'I don't know, but it sounds better than penicillin, doesn't it? I might go to the doctor more often if that's the kind of thing they're offering.'

Tony puffs out his chest and bellows across the room, 'I'm the only doctor you need, you skanky whore!'

Carol can only assume this is what passes for sweet nothings in their household. While Mandy giggles and tops up her own drink, Carol moves to the window and prays for rain. Not just rain, but something cataclysmic that will wash away the entire house. She can imagine watching as Tony and Mandy are swept away by raging waters, Tony shouting over the noise that there's still time for anal sex.

She wants to go home and look after Bob – still a novel impulse – but is under strict instructions to give no hint of a crisis. 'You've got to enjoy yourself,' was his solemn command.

Even at the best of times, that would have been a challenge, but today of all days it feels impossible. She can see the barbecue in the gloom of the back garden; an altar on which the evening will shortly be offered up as a burnt sacrifice, everyone chewing meat that will somehow manage to be both blackened and raw.

'Smile,' shouts Mandy, camera in hand. For a split second, Carol is blinded by a flash of light, and she wonders if this is what it feels like to die.

Mandy peers at the captured image. 'You crossed your

fingers,' she says, though from her tone it's hard to tell whether she thinks this is a good or a bad thing.

'Oh, that,' replies Carol, dismissively. 'It's just a habit.'

'You are a funny one.' She puts the camera down with clear relief, as though interfacing with technology exhausts her both mentally and physically. 'Now, back to the real business of the evening.' She hands Carol a large cocktail. 'We can't have you standing around sober.'

'Well, if you insist.' She takes several large mouthfuls.

'Hey, we'll have to watch this one!' shouts Tony. He points at her with a still-frozen pork chop. 'She's a woman on a mission, I can tell. This is what happens when a man stays at home to scratch his nuts.'

In the mind-numbing inebriation that follows the barbecue, Mandy and Tony decide to turn on the disco lights in their living room, instantly making the house feel like a two-star karaoke lounge.

'It's great, isn't it?' shouts Mandy, as the lights sweep across the room and momentarily make her blonde highlights look like St Elmo's fire. 'It's just a shame nobody else could make it.'

'As impossible as it seems,' says Carol, her voice beginning to slur in direct proportion to her new-found honesty, 'maybe they didn't fancy a barbecue on a cold, damp night.'

'But it's fun, don't you think?'

'No, not really, but some of the food was actually okay. Though, of course, the alcohol helped.'

Mandy appears to take this as a compliment. 'I think maybe me and Tone are just outdoorsy types, you know what I mean? Not everyone's like us.'

'Jesus, Mandy, you're only outdoorsy in the sense that you park your car in the driveway rather than the garage!' She takes a large gulp of vodka. 'I need to go.'

'But you can't, not yet. I haven't told you our big news. Me and Tone are going to try for a baby.'

'Oh, dear God . . .' She takes another large mouthful of alcohol. 'I actually think the two of you should be considering sterilization.'

'Oh, don't worry about that. I already wipe all the door knobs with bleach.'

'What's that about knobs?' yells Tony, from the other side of the room.

'I wipe them with bleach, don't I? I've become a bit of a neat freak in my old age.'

'There's only one knob that matters in this house, and your mouth does just fine.'

'Okay,' says Carol. 'I definitely have to go.'

Mandy puts on a sad puppy-dog face, but a sudden burst of strobe lights make it look more like demonic possession.

'I want to write to a friend before I go to bed,' Carol shouts over the music. 'If I don't go now, I won't even be able to hold a pen, let alone think straight.'

'It's quicker if you use your fingers. I mean, I only type with two, but that's better than pecking at the keyboard with a biro.'

It occurs to Carol that if they were both men she might punch Mandy at this point. Instead she takes a deep breath, her head full of violent thoughts. 'Thank you,' she says, 'I might give that a try.'

32

TODAY COULD BE the day, Albert tells himself. Today could be the day that another letter arrives from Connie.

If he's honest, though, he knows that today is just as likely not to be the day. From a statistical perspective, he isn't even sure whether the passing days make it more or less likely he'll receive another letter. What if she's got bored of writing? Or what if she's dead? No amount of waiting will improve the chances of getting another letter then.

In the meantime he has to stay strong, he understands that. There are his lungs to consider, but he still isn't sure what he can do about them. The only thing he can really control is his mind. And he's determined to whip it into shape.

'You what?' says Mickey, when Albert tries to explain what he's doing.

'It's called Sudoku,' says Albert, hoping to sound as if he understands the subject thoroughly.

'And what language is that, then?'

'Does it matter? It's about the mental exercise.'

'Yeah, but what if the name means something important?'

'Look, the game's about numbers, not words.' He feels entitled to sound irritated, though in truth he's relieved for the distraction: the Sudoku puzzles he's tried so far have all been too hard to finish.

'Okay, numbers.' Mickey nods blankly. 'And why are you doing it?'

'Because it's good, isn't it? Keeps you sharp.'

'What – so you're worried you're becoming a bit blunt in your old age?'

'That's not what I said.'

'Yeah, but I've never seen you doing this stuff before.' He flicks through some of the other pages, a graveyard of unfinished attempts. 'And it looks like you're struggling with it, to be honest.'

'Is that the time?' says Albert. He snatches the book from Mickey's hands and tosses it to one side. 'That's the trouble with these things – you just lose track of the hours.'

'Maybe that's your age too, Albert. My mum was always forgetting what day it was. We used to think it was funny at first, but then she tried to use her hairdryer in the bathtub. May she rest in peace.'

Albert allows what he hopes is a respectful pause. 'I presume you're here to give me today's mail?'

'See, I'm getting as senile as you are! And I'm not even old.' He hands Albert a small bundle of letters. 'You know what, Albert? If there are any pages in that puzzle book you don't touch, could you rip them out and leave them in the

Gents? It's always nice to have something to pass the time when things get, you know, bunged up. I don't know if it's too much fibre or not enough, but nothing seems to move for days sometimes.'

He waits, presumably so Albert can share his thoughts on the subject.

They look at each other in silence.

'Okay, then,' says Mickey, 'cheerio.'

As soon as he's gone, Albert starts flicking through the envelopes excitedly.

Some improperly addressed business letters.

An illegible postcard.

Another letter for Santa, this one undoubtedly from a loathsome child with too much pocket money.

And then there it is.

A smiley face.

He tosses everything else into the bin. The only thing he wants is right here in his hands.

He nods approvingly at her choice of paper, so thick and creamy it feels warm to the touch. 'Expensive,' he says, barely able to disguise his pleasure.

He gently tears it open, savouring the moment with all the relish of someone getting a letter from a dear old friend.

33

Another letter! 'And so soon,' I hear you say.

Albert is unnerved by the words, but decides it's just her sarcasm. She's a Connie, after all.

I'm drunk again—

'That girl's got a drinking problem,' he says to himself. 'She won't be getting any liqueur chocolates for Christmas.'

—but don't worry, I'm not going to start screaming at you. That other time was unhappy-drunk . . . more like wailing-banshee-drunk, actually . . . but this time, well, I can't say I'm happy-drunk because my husband was diagnosed with cancer today. I don't love him, it's true, but I'm not completely heartless. I think I'm numb-drunk. I've been numbing the shock of his cancer. Though I've also been numbing the anguish of going to

143

a friend's barbecue. (FRIEND!!! Please shoot me now.)

Just for the record, I didn't plan to attend a party the same day my husband found out he had cancer. He was actually the one who insisted I go, so what could I do? When someone's just been told they have a deadly disease, you can't say no to the first thing they ask. Though I suppose there is a limit to how far you could take that statement. I mean, if he'd asked me to do something illegal or really perverse, I might have had to consider it. Fortunately my husband isn't that interesting.

I should probably clarify here that, strictly speaking, it's one of my husband's testicles that has cancer, not him. And since that particular testicle is now sitting in a fridge somewhere in Chelsea, you could say he doesn't have cancer at all. It's just no one knows that yet, and the alternative is that he HAS got cancer and then . . . fuck.

I mean, FUCK!!!!!

I don't even know what happens then.

Anyway, this letter is really a sort of set-the-record-straight confessional. Or maybe I'm just feeling guilty about what I said in my last letter.

You see, I know I've said I don't love my husband and I'm leaving him, etc., etc. (all of which is true by the way) but that doesn't mean I don't love him in broader, more general terms. It's sort of like . . . like being on a plane. My love for him is definitely not up in First Class with a glass of champagne and a good book. It's not even in an exit row in Economy (though I can see that the imagery might be appropriate). My love for him is actually in the middle of a cramped row at the very back of the plane, right next to the toilets. But at least it's onboard. That's surely all that matters.

So it's odd, although I don't love LOVE him (in that First-Class, leather-seats sort of way), the cancer has reminded me of the things I do love about him. It's not that I suddenly find myself thinking of all his sweet mannerisms and funny jokes, because he doesn't really have any sweet mannerisms and his jokes are pretty lame, to be honest. I suppose what I mean is we have a shared history. We have a child! It's like we've sailed through a massive storm together and we somehow survived. (Am I confusing you with all this talk of planes and ships? I'm confusing myself.) Let's just say our marriage was a very, very long flight and now the plane has crashed. The fact that I regretted getting on the plane, hated most of the journey, and now find myself in a place I don't want to be doesn't seem to matter any more. The point is, we survived. It's hard not to feel a bond with someone when you've been through an experience like that.

Though I suppose this metaphor doesn't really make sense because he doesn't even know the plane's crashed. As far as he's concerned, we've just hit a spot of turbulence but by tomorrow morning we'll be having breakfast on the beach. I know everything in life is subjective, but it would be hard for two people on the same flight to experience it THAT differently:

one of them buzzing along at 40,000 feet while the other stumbles through smoking wreckage.

God, I'm tired.

And I don't mean you're God, by the way. Even if He existed, I wouldn't be talking to that sod.

And you're not Richard, either, I know that. I won't be calling you Richard again, that was just a fleeting moment of madness.

Albert reads the sentence several times, still confused.

And I definitely won't be giving you my name again. That was one-time-only, I'm afraid.

Fortunately I've grown quite fond of the mystery and anonymity of C.

So here it is again,

C.

Albert sits in stunned silence. He's surrounded by missing letters, thousands of them, and yet he knows what's happened to hers.

She'd spoken from the heart, that's what it sounded like. She'd given him her name!

And it was thrown away.

Recycled as loo roll, along with a bunch of worthless junk.

He wants to shout, to scream, even cry.

Instead, as he sits there in the dusty silence, only one word softly bubbles to his lips.

'Fuck.'

34

CAROL IS CONFUSED. In the past two days, she's become oddly protective of Bob so that she finds herself worrying about his welfare even as she wonders how much longer it will be until she can break his heart. Her hangover from Mandy's barbecue has also brought them closer: as far as Bob is concerned, she didn't get drunk, she took one for the team.

It helps, of course, that sex is out of the question. Bob's scrotum still has the tender quality of a recent accident victim and he's made several references to having lost his sex drive – yet another thing he and Carol now have in common.

'This feels like the early days,' says Bob, as they snuggle beneath a blanket.

Carol laughs. 'No, you were much more randy in the early days!'

'I was only trying to keep you satisfied.'

'Oh, I see. Very generous of you! Very giving!'

'You seemed to enjoy it.'

She blushes and remembers brief, distant days when she had enjoyed sex with him; a time when he seemed to light up her world. It was only in later years she realized this wasn't testament to Bob's luminosity but, rather, the darkness of her own existence.

'Do you still love me?' he says.

The words hang in the air.

'Of course I love you.' Back row, near the toilets. 'Why do you ask?'

'It's just . . . I don't know, the years change people, don't they?'

'And we've had years.'

'Do you think we've changed?'

'Of course we have. I mean, we've got Sophie and all the stuff families are supposed to have. An overpriced house, a neglected garden, a lifetime of debt.'

'But I mean us.'

Carol doesn't like where this is going. She's enjoying the intimacy with Bob precisely because it isn't really intimacy. It's a theatrical portrayal of the real thing: a woman who's so good at pretending to be in love that her husband actually believes it. Bob is destroying the purity of the moment. Like the ring of a mobile phone in the stalls, there's no room in Carol's performance for the truth of everyday life.

'Where are all these questions coming from?' she says.

Just in case she sounds too confrontational, she gives him an affectionate belly rub. For a brief moment, even she has the feeling she's treating him like a dog. *I've thrown you a bone, now fetch.*

'I suppose getting sick makes you think about stuff like this,' he says. 'Makes me think about what I've accomplished.'

Carol can only imagine this is a depressing experience, because in truth he hasn't really accomplished much at all. Yes, they have a child, but that's more cause-and-effect, and yes, they have a decent car and a pleasant house, but none of it strikes Carol as the kind of thing a person could look on with any great sense of pride. If anything, it's a world of invisible poverty, where the houses and the cars give the impression of success, but with no substance beneath. If this is success, why does it require constant, mind-numbing work just to stand still?

'Do you think Sophie suspects anything?' says Bob.

Carol resists the urge to say that Sophie's too self-absorbed for that. 'She may think we're acting a bit strangely, but we're her parents: she probably expects us to be strange.'

Bob looks reassured.

'Are you sure you're okay to come tomorrow?' he says. 'You don't have to.'

She smiles at him, relieved that she can speak from the heart again.

'I've already told you, I want to. From now on, we're in this together.'

Carol immediately understands why people enjoy private medical care. The office of Bob's specialist has the feel of a members-only club, and for a moment she worries there might be a dress code.

'Yes,' she expects the receptionist to say, with a

condescending sneer. 'I know your husband has cancer, but until your hemline is below the knee you can both piss off.'

As it turns out, the receptionist is charming, with a manner suggestive of Swiss finishing schools and sprawling country estates. Even if they were paying for the experience themselves, Carol feels like they've already got their money's worth, and all this before meeting the doctor.

'Dr Fitzgerald will see you now,' says the receptionist, in perfectly enunciated vowels, and yet with such warmth that Carol can imagine them keeping in touch. Within weeks, she'll be getting regular invitations to pheasant shoots and debutante balls.

Bob's voice cuts through the vision: 'Carol? Carol?'

She realizes he's standing in front of her, his hand outstretched. He helps her up from the overstuffed armchair and leads her through to a mahogany-panelled consulting room where the doctor greets them with all the enthusiasm of long-lost friends.

'Mr Cooper,' he says, 'and this must be your lovely wife. It's such a pleasure to meet you.'

Short of offering them a martini or a quick round of bridge, he goes out of his way to make them comfortable. Coffee is brought in on expensive china, and their questions are patiently answered in a voice that makes cancer seem like a passing case of acne or a discreet wart. It will all be fixed in no time.

'I do want you to reconsider the implant we discussed,' he says, as he takes a small silicone cushion from his desk drawer. 'It would really be a very simple insertion and . . .' he holds it up and squeezes '. . . as you can see, it's engineered for a very lifelike effect.'

So this is what men do with their balls, thinks Carol. They squeeze them and admire their sponginess. She wonders whether they only do this in private or if they discuss it with their friends too. She's beginning to realize there may be many aspects of male bonding she's entirely misunderstood.

'Here,' says the doctor, excitedly. He hands the implant to Bob, clearly convinced that an opportunity to finger it will seal the deal.

'Is this the same as a breast implant?' Bob flashes a sideways glance at Carol as he says it.

'Er, yes, essentially. A breast would be considerably larger, of course, but the same basic consistency and feel.'

Bob starts massaging the implant with new-found fervour. From across the desk, the doctor begins to look repulsed and even Carol gets the feeling that Bob has regressed to some kind of prepubescent fantasy. She takes it from him and hands it back to the doctor with a long-suffering smile.

'So,' he says, quickly regaining his composure, 'if I may, I'd like you back at the hospital tomorrow for a full morning of blood tests and CT scans. Once we have the results of those, we'll know exactly where we stand.'

'And if it's bad news?'

'I never like to think of these things in terms of bad news. It's really a case of the distance we have ahead of us, whether this is a hundred-yard dash or a cross-country steeplechase.

Either way, I intend to welcome you across the finishing line with a firm handshake and a big fat gin.'

'You wouldn't get that on the NHS.'

'What – a doctor offering you gin?'

'No,' says Bob. 'I mean hope.'

'The way the NHS is, these days, you'd be lucky to get anything at all. You could be dead before you get what you need.' There's an awkward silence. 'Sorry, I didn't mean *you* could be dead.'

'Don't worry, I get it.'

'I meant, *one* could be . . .'

The clarification is wasted on Bob, and even though the grammar is correct, it sounds preposterous coming from Carol. She isn't a 'one' kind of person. It's a vaguely depressing realization that demography prevents her using her own language properly. She thinks of the receptionist and how she flits across words like a butterfly; always saying the right thing in just the right way and making it all sound so natural.

'She's a butterfly and I'm an elephant.'

'What was that?'

'Nothing. I was just thinking out loud.'

'About elephants?'

'No, about life.'

She glances down as they cross the Thames. Low-tide has left wide banks of mud on either side of the river, laying it bare and exposing what is better left unseen.

Discomforted by its raw honesty, Carol looks away,

focuses on the road ahead. Soon the streets of London will begin to look dirtier and more run-down, a sure sign they're heading south.

'Are you happy with your life?' she says.

'Happy with getting cancer and losing a testicle at forty-two? No, not especially, Carol.'

'I don't mean that. I mean . . .' she sighs, not completely sure what she means, '. . . happy with who you are, I suppose.'

As soon as she's said it, she realizes this is the wrong question to ask a man like Bob. It's possibly to his credit that he never ponders subjects like this. His happiness is an equation of simple things – whether to have another beer, how many times to badger Carol for sex before giving up – but everything else, all the big existential stuff, that's fixed and immutable.

He gives her a worried look. 'Why? Are you happy? With yourself, I mean?'

'Of course,' she says, a little too quickly. 'I don't even know why I mentioned it. Just ignore me.'

35

ALTHOUGH HE'S MISSED the chance to confirm her name, there's nothing about the most recent letter that changes Albert's suspicions. She's still acting like a Connie.

'Probably a gin drinker,' he says to himself, as he opens the biscuit tin and carefully places the new letter under the first. He wants them in sequence – a man can't work in the postal service for forty years and not appreciate letters arranged in a logical order – and he wants the smiley faces staring up at him whenever he opens the tin.

'It's not nice to hear her husband's sick,' he says to Gloria, as he opens a can of sardines and empties it on to a plate. 'And it's not really the kind of news that warrants a smiley face, is it? But she's already said she doesn't love him. And let's not forget she is a Connie.'

Eyes wide in expectation, Gloria watches as he slowly mashes the fish and then carries the plate towards her. Before he reaches her, however, Engelbert Humperdinck begins to pound through the walls, crooning so loudly that everything in the room seems to vibrate. Albert stops mid-stride, the plate still in his hand.

'He's at it again,' he says, with a sigh. Gloria licks her lips and struggles to move in her plaster cast, but Albert is too distracted to notice.

'It's not just music, is it? That's the trouble.' He starts to pace the room. 'It's a taunt, that's what it is. A challenge. Trying to make me go over there and knock on his door.'

He and Max both know there'll be no confrontation. Albert could always call the police, but unless he can be sure Max is going to be locked up and left to die in prison, he'd rather not deal with the consequences. The police officers would come, which is great, but then they'd go – and that's what makes Albert afraid. It's easier to pretend he's always liked Engelbert Humperdinck; to think of it as a free concert.

'He's always been a bit too syrupy for me, but at least it's a different song this time.' Engelbert launches back into the chorus, the volume so loud it's more like blunt trauma than music. 'Though I have to say, syrupy isn't the word that springs to mind right now.'

At long last he notices Gloria's desperation, a yearning so strong she's beginning to look possessed. 'You poor thing,' he says. 'Here you are.'

He puts the plate in front of her. She immediately starts gulping down the fish in frenzied mouthfuls, not even bothering to chew.

Albert watches for a few seconds, but the music is drowning the inevitable sound of her purr. Without that, there's no pleasure in it.

'Sorry,' he says, as he snatches the plate away, 'but we'll have to do this later.'

Entombed in plaster, Gloria can only bob her head forlornly as the plate sails back towards the kitchen.

'Don't worry, it'll be back before you know it.'

From next door, Engelbert lurches to a halt in the angry sound of a needle scraping across vinyl. There's a split second of silence, followed by the unmistakable sound of Max's voice.

'You bloody cow!' He struggles to find the start of the song again, Engelbert's crooning now reduced to random snatches of sound. 'Do that again and I'll throw your bloody frame out the window, you hear me?'

Moments later, the song restarts, the walls beginning to shake as Engelbert sweeps into the opening verse on a tsunami of noise. Yet barely a few seconds in, the needle gets stuck and the song becomes a chant, hypnotic in its repetition.

The sound stops, replaced by Max's voice, quieter this time, but angrier too.

'See what you've done? You fucking whore!'

Silence.

Albert waits to see if Max will try a different record, but he doesn't cope well with setbacks, Albert knows that. He's more likely to spend the next few hours scowling into a big glass of beer.

Free to enjoy his home in peace again, Albert carries the fish back to Gloria and listens happily now as she devours it with a contented purr.

36

THE NEXT DAY dawns to the kind of cold, grey weather that doubtless has people across London reaching for Prozac or jumping in front of trains.

'And it'll get much worse in the months to come,' says Bob, as he pulls on a coat and scarf. He says it with an earnest, hopeful expression, as though he needs to witness an environmental disaster to make sense of his own misfortune. 'They say it's going to be a long, hard winter.'

Carol has never been able to hear 'long' and 'hard' in the same sentence without thinking of sex. Not sex with Bob, of course, to whom neither adjective applies, but—

He rouses her from the fantasy with a kiss on the cheek. 'See you later.'

'Are you sure I can't come?'

'No, I'm just going to be scanned and prodded about. I don't even know if they'd let you in the room with me.'

Over the years, she's grown adept at reading between the lines, knowing when 'no' really means 'yes'. On this occasion, she decides he's being sincere.

'Well, call me if you change your mind,' she says. 'I'm going to meet Helen for coffee, but that's all.'

As Bob opens the front door, a chill wind blows through the house. 'Bloody hell,' he shouts.

He stands in the open doorway, the wind tugging at his scarf and ruffling the unopened bills on the hallway table.

'Yes, Bob, it's cold. Can you shut the door, please?'

Silence.

'For Christ's sake, Bo—' She rushes to the door and finds herself gobsmacked too. 'Christ . . .'

'Is it just me, or was that not there yesterday?'

In the front garden of the house opposite, a flagpole now towers over the cul-de-sac. Overhead, a tired-looking Union Jack billows at full mast.

'It's bloody enormous,' says Bob.

Carol stares at it, too confused to say anything. It almost seems an indictment of her life that something so striking could spring up unobserved.

'They surely need planning permission for something like that.'

'I don't know,' mumbles Carol.

'Well,' says Bob, at length, 'I should get going.'

'Yeah, see you,' she replies, still staring at the flagpole open-mouthed.

*

If London is in the grips of pre-winter blues, nobody has told Helen. She greets Carol with the sort of smile she's not worn in months, possibly even years.

'You look very pleased with yourself,' says Carol, unable to control the suspicion in her voice.

'Do I?' Helen blushes, useless at being coy. 'I have a date. Well, it's not really a date.'

'Then what is it?'

'Well, I suppose it is a date. But it's a first date, just a cup of coffee, actually, so it's more like a date that's pretending not to be a date.'

Unable to think of an appropriate response, Carol just stares at her, confounded.

'Well, there's no need to look like that,' says Helen. 'I do have a life, you know.'

'No, I'm not, I'm – I'm happy for you. It's just . . . I know this has nothing to do with your love life, but my neighbours have just put a flagpole in their front garden. It just appeared from nowhere. One day it wasn't there, the next day it was.' Helen looks confused as to where this is going. 'And now you're telling me you have a date. It's like I've fallen down a rabbit hole or something.'

'Is my life really that tragic?'

'No, it's just . . . Are we talking about a date with a real, live man?'

'No, Carol, I've borrowed the key to the local morgue. I find that corpses are underrated as potential life partners.'

'I mean is this a date-date, or . . . I don't know, just some guy hoping to sell you a time-share?'

Helen's stony silence suggests now is a good time to back-pedal.

'So, how did you meet him?' says Carol.

'I placed a personal ad.'

'Said the woman who believes in letting things just come to her.'

'The right man can never find me if I don't tell him where to look.'

She begins making tea, an elaborate ritual that involves emptying jars of foul-smelling herbs into her favourite glass teapot. She's explained on many occasions that the leaves have medicinal properties, though Carol has always seen that as a good reason not to serve them to guests.

'I hope you're aware,' says Carol, 'that men who surf personals only want sex.'

'Oh, please, all men want sex!' There's a faint smile on her lips, a hint of anticipation. 'Even the sensitive ones who say they want to settle down. It's very convenient that starting a family requires lots and lots of intercourse.'

She pours boiling water into the teapot and looks genuinely pleased as the water turns a brackish green.

'Anyway,' she says, as she carries it to the sofa, 'sex won't be happening yet because I want you to come too.'

'On your date?'

'That's what I've been trying to say. It's only a date in the getting-to-know-you sense.'

'And surely you could do that better if I wasn't around.'

'But you're my best friend. He can't get to know me without seeing me in context.'

160

This strikes Carol as a very strange approach to meeting someone new, like wanting him to smell her morning breath before she agrees to the first kiss.

'And what if he likes you,' says Carol, 'but doesn't like me?'

'Then sod him! He can find someone else.'

'Yeah, but I was thinking of you, not him.'

'Great, my best friend thinks I should just settle for the first man who shows some interest.'

'That's not what I meant.'

'If you must know, I got lots of replies to my ad.'

'From what kind of men?'

'Does it matter?'

'Well, if they were all over sixty, I don't think it counts.'

'They weren't *all* over sixty.'

'The rest were in prison.'

'Carol, will you come or not?'

'What happens if I say no?'

'Then I'll just trick you into it. Either way, you'll end up meeting him. I want to know what you think.'

Not knowing what state of mind Bob may be in when he gets home, Carol decides to fill the house with comfort food. This is her excuse, anyway. In reality, she just enjoys being at the supermarket. It's always been a Bob-free zone, and Sophie would sooner hang herself than do something as useful as shop for groceries.

She wanders the aisles, losing herself in the sheer excess of it all. To her eye, every item seems to tell a story, to suggest an existence different from her own. There's a certain pleasure in pondering how her life might have turned out if she was the kind of person who bought organic goat's milk or toasted sesame oil.

She's always found the herbs and spices worthy of a lingering visit. Under different circumstances, she can imagine buying fennel seeds and grinding them by hand until the whole house smells of aniseed. What she'd do with them then is less clear – and yet here they are, thirty or forty packets of fennel seeds waiting to be bought by the kind of people with a broader culinary repertoire, and spicier lives, than her.

It's tempting to imagine this is the real problem in her life: that if only she'd paid more attention to Nigella Lawson, everything would be different. Bob would doubtless be fatter, which isn't an appealing prospect, but Sophie . . . That could be what's missing in their relationship – mother and daughter cooking up a storm of lavish cakes and saucy little flans – the unpredictable process of baking now appearing to parallel the mysterious alchemy of human affection.

She wants to test her theory by waiting to see what kind of happy, fulfilled mothers come by, but it seems suspicious to just stand around in a supermarket. Wander aimlessly, by all means – it's perfectly plausible that half the people in here have been wandering around for months – but to stand and wait feels sinister, predatory. Besides which, what is she supposed to do when someone comes along? Introduce herself? Ask them for recipes? Tell them she needs a friend?

She goes to the next aisle, still secretly wishing she'd stayed.

If nothing else, this aisle offers lots of things she can actually buy: the kind of denatured, processed junk that commonly passes for food in her house. Wrapped in plastic and suffused with preservatives, it looks as if it could sit here fresh and tasty for ever. If this was Pompeii, archaeologists could dig it all up in millennia from now and eat most of it for lunch. And what does it say about Carol that this is what fills her cupboards?

Feeling guilty, she backtracks to the previous aisle and adds a packet of fennel seeds to her cart. Emboldened, she continues retracing her steps, picking up packets of baker's yeast and gelatine. The fact that she doesn't know how to use any of these things seems unimportant. All that matters is she's taking a stand.

At the end of the aisle she picks up a bar of dark chocolate, the kind that Bob and Sophie loathe. If she's honest, she doesn't much like it either, but at this moment it represents everything her own life is not. She throws a couple of bars into her trolley and heads back towards the spices, feeling more alive with every step.

Carol expects Bob to be a mess when he gets home, but he's almost blasé about his day.

'They need to do more tests,' he says. 'They think it was a very early-stage malignancy.'

Malignancy. It sounds strange to hear something so technical and polysyllabic coming from Bob's mouth, almost as shocking as the cancer itself.

'That's great,' says Carol. 'I mean, relatively speaking.'

'Though I think I'm coming down with the flu.'

Carol immediately feels her sympathy wane; can almost hear the engines shutting down. For the last eighteen years, Bob hasn't been able to sneeze without considering it flu, a process that always climaxes in elaborate self-medication and several days of sloth. Fortunately he appears too distracted by the shopping bags to dwell on it.

'Was there anything in the shop you didn't buy?'

His tone is more perplexed than impressed. Carol wants to reply that she only went to the supermarket for his sake, but that's hard to claim when most of her purchases are things he'll never eat.

'I mean, dark chocolate is bad enough,' he says, 'but with chilli flakes?' He grimaces, the mere mention of it enough to induce nausea. 'And what are we supposed to do with these?'

He holds up a bag of cardamom pods. Even Carol is unsure about those, but she was moved by the aroma coming through the plastic: the scent of Indian temples and the chaotic backstreets of Delhi.

'Did you manage to buy anything I can actually eat?'

Carol rummages through one of the bags and pulls out a pack of glazed doughnuts. 'They're just junk,' she says. 'There's nothing in them that's good for you.'

'But at least I won't throw up on myself after eating one.'

Carol opens a jar of sundried tomatoes and breathes in their fragrance: Sicily, late summer, the whole island shimmering in a heat haze.

'I'm feeling a bit headachy,' says Bob, through a mouthful

of doughnut. He takes a second and third from the packet, holding them in sugar-dusted fingers. 'I'm going to lie down on the sofa for a while.'

'I think I'll make something new for dinner.' Bob doesn't appear to hear her. 'It'll be . . . a surprise.'

An hour later, Bob has managed to make the entire living room feel like the infectious ward of a tropical hospital. Overheated, dimly lit and tangy with the scent of body odour, the room is suggestive of a man with much greater problems than cancer.

'I don't think it's healthy to have it this hot in here,' says Carol, from the doorway.

Bob is visible in the gloom only by the light from the television. As he cranes his neck to look at her, it gives him a bluish, lifeless appearance. 'I think it's better to sweat it out,' he says.

'But maybe not a great idea to sweat it into the sofa.' Bob ignores her, turns back to the television. 'Dinner's almost ready.'

'What is it?'

Carol hesitates, unsure how to answer the question without putting him off. 'Give me a few more minutes and you can see for yourself.'

37

ALBERT CAN FEEL the change. It's crept up on him subtly, but there's no doubting the truth of it. And he knows Gloria can sense it too. She's looking at him differently; seems to know she has to share his affections with yet another woman.

Still, he reassures himself he isn't becoming obsessed, not like last time. Back then he couldn't think straight, couldn't eat for want of a letter, but now – it's true he's longing to hear from Connie again, but he and Connie have become friends, and that's what friends do when they haven't heard from one another. They worry.

'Do you think she's all right?'

Gloria blinks cryptically, her plastered legs sticking out in front of her like something mummified, an ancient Egyptian idol. And she's worthy of worship, thinks Albert, this cat who understands everything but never speaks.

'I wonder if Connie would be the kind of person to hug? She certainly sounds it. I mean, despite all her problems, she's obviously got a good heart.' Gloria closes her eyes, his voice a soporific. 'It's been a long time since I had a hug . . .'

By the time Albert's ready to leave for work, the uncertainty of not knowing if today will be The Day is beginning to weigh on his mind. More importantly, he's one day closer to retirement, and what if he hasn't heard from her before then? He won't be able to pop in and check the mail after that. All contact will be lost.

Burdened by the thought, he's mentally ill-prepared to find Max outside having a smoke.

'Uh-oh,' says Max, 'who's died now? It's not the cat, is it? Because I don't want you going out for the day with a corpse in there. It'll attract flies.'

'The cat's fine.'

'Of course it's not fine, you fucking idiot! It's got two broken legs and a brain the size of a pea.' He watches as Albert trudges away, his head hanging low. 'Even your cat's a hopeless cripple. You should really stop and ask yourself what that says about you.'

Winter's approach feels as though someone has punched a hole in the sky and all the light, warmth and colour are quickly draining away. Everything about the weather speaks to Albert of finality and loss, a meteorological expression of his darkest fears.

When he eventually gets to work, it's with a heavy heart and a desperate need to talk to someone, anyone.

'How are you?' says Darren, as he strides by, clearly not intending it as a question.

'I'm worried about a friend, actually.'

Darren stops. 'Sorry, what did you say?'

'I'm worried about a friend. I've not heard from her in a while.'

Darren looks uncomfortable with this kind of intimacy, unsure what to say now that everyday etiquette has broken down.

'Well, maybe you should give her a call.'

'I don't have her number.'

'Then pay her a visit, perhaps.'

'I, er . . . I can't remember her address.'

Darren nods, the situation clear at last: this isn't Albert worrying about a friend, it's Albert losing his mind.

'I wish I could help, I really do, but you know how it is.' He taps his watch and scurries away.

Albert spends the next five hours alone with a few sacks of unwanted mail and a small, barred window full of grey clouds. It's only after lunch that one of his youngest colleagues wanders in with today's undeliverable mail. Even lost in the pile, Carol's letter is instantly recognizable – the edges of the paper are warm to the touch, a hug for the fingertips. Before the young man has even left the room, Albert tosses everything else to one side and sits there staring at Carol's envelope. Its smiley face is everything he needs at this moment, everything the day and the week haven't been.

Wanting to make the feeling last, he decides he won't open it straight away, but will instead wait until he gets home, the rest of his day now sparkling with a delicious anticipation.

38

I am a bad person. I probably should have realized this some time ago – I have, in fact, had my suspicions for most of my life. But now, at the age of thirty-eight, it has been confirmed once and for all in high-definition. It's like I've only ever seen my shortcomings on some crappy videotape, and now I'm watching them on Blu-ray. It takes self-loathing to a whole new level.

The problem is this: my husband (the father of my daughter, the man with one testicle) has just gone to bed with what he claims is flu. I should be nursing him. I mean, he may have cancer, for Christ's sake. I should be walking on water and raising the dead in my efforts to make him feel comfortable. But you know what? I don't care. I don't mean I don't care about the cancer, because I do, but I definitely don't care about the flu. I don't even believe he has flu. I think it's a sort of elaborate pity-me moment. Does he not think cancer is enough?

See? I'm doing it again. There are people who donate money to charity to help people like my husband, and here am I (his wife!!) doubting his motives and thinking how much I loathe the sight of him.

If this doesn't make me a bad person, I'm not sure what does. I can see that murder is considerably worse, but perhaps this is where it all starts, with a simmering resentment of a man who's just lost a testicle.

Dinner didn't help. I was trying to be creative. Actually, that's not true. Creative makes me sound like someone with artistic pretensions. I was actually trying to be someone else. I'm not sure why I think that's better than aspiring to creativity. Right there, that probably says everything you need to know about me.

I suppose in broad terms I was trying to be Nigella Lawson. At the very least I was trying to be someone who feels at ease with food. You know, the kind of person who can go to the cupboard and knock together something amazing from whatever she finds. So that was me, throwing together all sorts of wonderful things in the belief that I wouldn't just create a fabulous dinner, I'd also miraculously change my life – that the simple act of conjuring up good food would make me a different woman and transform my husband into a completely different man.

It didn't work out like that. And, just for the record,

cardamom and basil don't make a great combination. Especially with lemon zest. And fennel seeds tend to get stuck in your teeth, particularly when you have to chew through sinewy strips of dried beef.

To my husband's credit, at no point did he say he didn't like it. He just pecked at it and said he'd never thought of matching those flavours before. To be honest, neither had I. I just thought I was being spontaneous and carefree, though in retrospect I can see why Nigella didn't come up with that recipe.

What I'm trying to say is, I'm not surprised he didn't like it. I cooked it and even I hated it. What I take exception to is his reaction: a little prodding with his fork, some half-hearted bites and a lot of sniffing. I think I would have preferred it if he'd thrown his plate across the room, maybe started smashing some other stuff too. A good fight's like a thunderstorm, don't you think? Really clears the air.

I have this fantasy—

Carol stops, unsure if she really wants to run the risk of her most private thoughts being read by a total stranger. Deciding that it doesn't count when you don't know who they are, she continues.

I have this fantasy where I'm the wife of a tall, dark Italian. He's impossibly sexy, of course, with everything man-sized, if you know what I mean. And he's a passionate, hot-blooded male. When we argue,

171

he wants to hit me, I can see it in his eyes, but there's his mother and the village priest to think of, so he just smashes things. The framed photographs are first to go, then the crockery, plate after plate all smashed to pieces, while I scream back at him, set fire to his clothes and throw them into the street (none of this is very practical from a financial perspective, I appreciate that, but let's just assume we have plenty of money for replacements). When we've exhausted ourselves with smashing and screaming, and the entire town is outside listening to the commotion, we fuck like animals, on every surface in the house, unable to stop until we're drenched in sweat and sore to the touch.

I think I've said too much.

For now,

C.

Albert puts the letter down, his face a shade paler than before.

'If this is how she talks to a complete stranger, I wonder what she's like with her friends.' He glances at Gloria, embarrassed to have read the letter in her presence. 'Maybe it's just as well I don't have her address – I really wouldn't know how to reply to something like that.'

He takes the letter to the biscuit tin and carefully places it inside, smiley face up.

'Though I suppose I wouldn't have to mention it, would I? I could just talk about her husband being sick. It's never nice to hear someone's feeling poorly.'

He stands straighter now, as if his whole body has caught a breeze and is beginning to fill with air.

'I mean, I can't send it to her, it's true, but I can still reply. And it's almost the same in the end, don't you think? Most people don't listen when I talk anyway, so what's the difference?'

He notices Gloria staring at him.

'No, you're right. It's childish, isn't it?' His shoulders sag again, the moment lost. 'Connie's allowed to write letters because she's an emotional girl with a drinking problem. Lively imagination too.' He blushes and tries to wipe her words from his mind. 'Someone like Connie writes because she needs all the help she can get. Our job is just to listen, isn't it?'

Yet even Gloria notices how his voice lacks conviction, and that he lingers over the open biscuit tin with an almost palpable sense of longing.

39

His name is Ricky, and he obviously didn't know that a friend would be joining him and Helen on their non-date date.

After the initial confusion has passed, Carol is sure she can see excitement building in his eyes; that maybe this is Helen's roundabout way of suggesting a threesome. Not that Ricky seems the type to be invited on threesomes, which is presumably why he's looking so excited.

Carol wonders if she should make a reference to Bob, but she suspects Ricky would just take it as confirmation that they're suburban swingers up for a good time. She can imagine him having some kind of haemorrhage, the enormity of it all too much to handle.

Curiously, Helen makes no attempt to speak; evidently thinks that the best way to get to know Ricky is simply to observe him in conversation with Carol, and sometimes to ignore both of them completely.

Faced with Helen's silence and Ricky's confusion, Carol finds herself asking the kind of questions that make the occasion seem more like an interview than a social event.

'So, what line of work are you in?'

'Medical sales. I basically visit hospitals and sell them things.'

'And do they actually find that useful or do they think you're a bit of a double-glazing salesman?'

'No,' he says, clearly hurt. 'It's all important stuff. And they get a good price.' He glances at Helen, perhaps in the hope of drawing her into the conversation. 'So if ever you need a catheter or a colostomy bag, I'm your man.'

On a scale of one to ten, this doesn't strike Carol as inspired sweet-talk.

'Have you been single for long?' she says. Her tone implies she already knows the answer, that it's painfully apparent – not just to her, but to everyone else in the café too, even passing motorists.

'Yeah,' he says, 'a while.'

An awkward silence falls across the table and Ricky begins to look glum. Helen, meanwhile, demurely sips her non-dairy chai latte, seemingly unaware that the whole date is disintegrating in mid-air.

Left with nothing else, Carol ploughs on: 'So, do you live round here?'

'No, I'm in Milton Keynes.'

Milton Keynes.

Carol wants to ask why he would drive two hours just for a non-alcoholic drink with a woman like Helen – had he not seen her pictures in advance? Instead she just smiles politely. 'I don't know Milton Keynes very well.'

'It's nice.'

And there we have it. Any man who can like Milton Keynes would naturally find Helen attractive. As much as Carol loves her as a friend, she knows that Helen is the romantic equivalent of a bland commuter town; the kind of place that isn't perfect but people put up with it because the houses are within their budget.

This naturally raises the question of what kind of place Carol herself is. There was a time when she would have said she was a factory that had been zoned for demolition. Since Bob's illness, she feels more like an impact crater, the final resting place of a meteor that's wiped out all life within a thousand-mile radius.

'Carol?' says Helen. And again, louder, 'Carol?'

She realizes Helen and Ricky are staring at her with the worried look of people witnessing a psychotic episode. 'Sorry, I was miles away.'

'Carol's a dreamer,' says Helen, with a nervous smile.

'The world needs dreamers,' says Ricky.

'Thank you,' replies Carol. 'I don't think the world needs any more middle-aged women staring at walls, but it's a kind thing to say.'

They both laugh.

Carol glances at him, then looks away, suddenly aware that she's blushing.

'You were flirting.'

'I was not.'

'Carol.'

'I'm married.'

'To a man you're planning to leave.'

'Yes, and the last thing I want to do is find another loser.'

'Great. And what if I liked him?'

'No, look, he's nice.'

'For a loser?'

'I just mean – he lives in Milton Keynes!'

'So if he moved to Wimbledon, let's say, you'd sleep with him?'

'No!'

'I saw you blushing.'

'That was . . . purely hormonal, nothing to do with me.'

They walk across the park, its trees shedding their leaves in a final, frantic burst of self-destruction.

'I'm not sure I want to see him again anyway,' says Helen. 'It's a bit like swimming. I always want to do it until I get to the pool. Then I look at all the water and think, Sod that.' She sighs gently, could almost be letting the air out of her hopes. 'Maybe I've just been alone too long. Ricky was nice, but it all seems like too much effort.'

'You were the one who placed the personal ad.'

'True, but now I think I'd rather just use a vibrator and live the rest of my life in peace.'

'Maybe that's what you should tell Ricky. "It was nice to meet you, but I prefer the Duracell Bunny."'

'I might, actually. I don't see why I should build my life around a man.'

'Perhaps because you want to get laid by something that can actually cuddle you afterwards.'

'But that doesn't have to be a man, does it?' She speaks at the ground now; at the trees and the dead leaves blowing in the wind, anything but Carol. 'I mean . . . we could be secret lovers. You and me.' Self-consciousness makes the words come out too quickly, all her fluidity of movement gone. 'It's supposed to be the highest form of lovemaking. Two women, no aggressor.'

'Wouldn't we have to be attracted to each other first?' Helen looks offended. 'I don't mean you're not attractive. I just find myself gravitating more to . . . well, you know . . . cock.'

'Of course, I was only—'

'And I know that! And I love you for suggesting it, really I do! I mean, that's surely what an old friend is for.' Worrying that she put too much stress on 'friend', she links her arm in Helen's. 'And anyway, look at us, we're already like an old married couple.'

'I just want you to know you can still find happiness here. You don't have to leave Bob.'

Carol laughs, assumes she's joking.

'I mean,' continues Helen, 'you don't have to destroy your family life—'

'My really satisfying family life.'

'—just to go looking for something you may never find. Maybe it's better to be grateful for what you have.'

Carol lets go of her arm on the pretence of rearranging her scarf.

'Bob loves you,' says Helen.

'Oh, please. Bob's only definition of love is regular

sex, though on that basis alone he's clearly not in a loving relationship.' She puts her hands into her pockets and continues walking, a gap slowly opening up between them. 'You're the one who's always talking about truth and honesty. What about hope? And optimism?'

'I'm just trying to be realistic. Sometimes it's better to compromise—'

'Give up.'

'Compromise . . . and accept that some of what you want is better than spending the rest of your life looking for more but never finding it.'

40

Do you ever get the feeling that no one is listening? I don't mean that they're ignoring you. I mean, that no one is *listening*. That they only hear what they want to hear.

My best friend (God, that expression sounds so juvenile right now) – 'my closest friend' has just told me I'd be better off settling for chronic, soul-destroying disappointment rather than risk venturing off and only making things worse. Has she not been listening to anything I've said for, oh, the last ten or twenty years?

There are two ways of looking at her advice. One, she's depressed and she's transferring her lack of hope onto me. If you knew her, you'd realize this is very likely.

So that's one possibility. But it's also possible she's simply looking at my track record in life and deciding I'd be better off not trying to make any more decisions. And I can see her point: let's not forget, I'm the woman who thought it was a good idea to marry a man I didn't love. I think if I had a friend like me, I'd probably tell her to stop making decisions too. I think the human race should be relieved that there's no way for a middle-aged woman in Croydon to accidentally destroy all life on the planet. I'd be a danger to us all.

I like writing to you. You just quietly absorb everything I have to say, no interruptions, no judgemental facial tics. The odd thing is, even if all these letters are being tossed in the bin unread, that's okay. For the first time in my life, I can actually relate to religious people. In the absence of proof, I'm free to believe whatever I want to believe. And I choose to believe you read everything I write. You hear me. You understand. You even nod approvingly and occasionally blush.

I suppose on this occasion I'm writing because I'm tired. I don't mean in the literal sense, though I wouldn't say no to a nap. I'm just tired of being me.

It's a bit like driving a car. Before you learn to drive, it all looks so easy. Then you get behind the wheel and spend the next three weeks stalling the engine. Well, that's me, but I've been doing it for thirty-eight years. I still haven't figured out the clutch control of life and now I want to stop, give the keys back, let somebody else drive.

That's what my mother's religion is, a bus for people who've given up trying to drive themselves. It's a bus with hard seats and dirty windows, but everybody's so demoralized by trying to do hill starts and reverse parking, they all think they're better off on board.

I'm rambling, aren't I? What a surprise.

My dad didn't want me to marry – have I ever mentioned that? I don't mean he wanted me to stay single for life. It wasn't one of those 'Get thee to a nunnery' moments. He just thought my husband-to-be was a dickhead. He knew I could do better. And that's through the blurred lens of a lifelong drinking problem.

Drinking was always his big problem. Ironically, I get the feeling that sobriety is mine. It's like I can't say what I really mean unless my conscious mind is knocked out first. That can't be a good sign.

Would you like to know something no one else knows? Whenever someone takes a photo of me, I cross my fingers. I would call it a habit, but that's not true. A habit is something you do without thinking. This is more like a ritual. It's my way of saying, 'There's more to me than this' – that the picture tells only half the story. I suppose it's really my way of saying, 'I exist' – which is, of course, entirely for my own benefit. As far as I'm aware, other people don't doubt my existence. It's only me who seems to feel ghostly, like I'm haunting other people's lives rather than living my own.

Do you know what? Bollocks to this. Who says I can't leave my husband now? And who says he even has cancer? His left testicle had cancer, but that's gone.

It's probably been sold to a kebab factory by now. Problem solved.

Maybe it's the wine talking (I've only had four glasses, though it's four more than I should have had), but I'm going to tell him tomorrow. I would tell him now, but he's asleep upstairs (with a fever – turns out he did have flu. Oops). As evil as I am, I'm not the kind of person to wake him up just so I can say, 'I'm leaving you.' He wouldn't make much sense anyway. He's never been good at waking up. We can add that to his list of failings.

So for now it's our secret, just yours and mine.

I would ask you what you think, but thankfully I only have the feeling you absorb my words. I haven't started hearing your voice too. (Frankly, I've never understood why everyone admires Joan of Arc. The woman was a certifiable nutcase.)

We have an obligation to be true to ourselves, don't you think? I've failed at that for as long as I can remember, mostly for really crap reasons. But we have to be honest when we're not happy with life, otherwise we turn into – well, me, basically.

It's everyone's right to live happily. Mine. Yours. Even that man I can hear snoring upstairs (which also means he's drooling on his pillow, never a pretty sight).

I like you, damn it, and I want you to be happy, too. So be brave. Demand more!

C.

Albert lingers over the last paragraph, reads it again and again, the smile on his face growing so broad and heartfelt that even Gloria begins to purr.

41

It's more than rubbish. In its own way it's a testament to the solitary existence of a lonely old man. And the bag holding it all together is nothing but a flimsy bin liner, the kind that had seemed really good value when Albert found them in the supermarket. It was only when he got them home that he realized they were fit for nothing but being thrown away – presumably in a stronger, more expensive brand.

Aware that the bag may rip and tear at any moment, Albert walks slowly past Max's flat – no sign of the man himself, just a lingering sense of evil, a deathly halo of radioactivity. There's no need to rush: he still has plenty of time to get to work.

He's nearing the rubbish chute when the lift doors open and out steps Max with his morning paper.

'Why are you skulking about?' he barks.

Albert flinches.

The bag breaks.

Anyone watching its contents scatter in the wind would

quickly conclude that Albert is prone to certain medical problems. Everything else suggests a diet not of food so much as food-like substances, all heavily processed and thick with sugar.

'Having a little trouble with your back passage?' says Max, as he kicks at an empty tube of Preparation-H. 'Been sticking things up there, have you? You filthy bugger! Though better you do it to yourself than some poor choir boy.'

He watches as Albert scrambles to collect it, the wind tugging at his clothes.

'And that doesn't look like a very healthy diet.' A plastic wrapper still smeared with synthetic cream flies over the parapet and out across the roofs of London. 'Is that the kind of crap you used to feed your wife? No wonder she's dead.'

The words hit Albert so hard, he isn't even aware of Max walking away, and as for the welling of his eyes, that could just be the chill wind.

He struggles to stand upright, feels older and stiffer than he ever has before. There's still rubbish on the ground, but this is South London: nobody will care.

Unable to get far, he shuffles into the stairwell and takes a seat on the grimy steps. All around him, the walls are graffitied with successive generations of angry statements, so that to sit here is to witness the evolution of society – from the heady days when 'Down With School' was considered subversive to the more recent 'Death to Homo Bastards' and 'Fuck You Nigger Cunts'. Albert tries not to read them, but it's hard. He has to look at something or he'll go mad. If he closes his eyes he can only see the morning everything changed; the morning he woke up to find his wife dead beside him. And, cutting through all his memories, the sound of Max's sneering voice, the only thing in his life that has survived the years intact.

He can hear Max watering his plants out on the walkway. At least on a day like this, with a cold wind blowing, he'll be in no hurry to linger outside.

Albert still can't comprehend how a man like Max finds any pleasure in plants; how someone so unkind can want to nurture another living thing. It's like hearing that Hitler loved to cuddle puppies, or always cried during reruns of *Lassie*.

The clunk of Max's front door rouses him from his thoughts. Moving quietly, cautiously, he peers out at the walkway. No one in sight.

On tiptoe now, Albert makes his way home, unlocking his front door with all the stealth of a ninja, and closing it so gently that even Gloria sleeps undisturbed.

Albert knows there's no point calling in sick. Today of all days he doesn't need to hear Darren implying that he's irrelevant and useless. 'Yeah, take as much time as you need. Your presence here is pointless anyway.'

He wants to take his wife's things out of the wardrobe, to touch them, to hold them, but he can't do that to himself. Not again. The momentary relief is nothing compared to the pain that follows; the realization that a few time-worn garments are all that remain of a loving woman, their only scent of age and decay.

Instead he goes to the biscuit tin and takes out Connie's letters. He lingers over each one, not reading them so much as losing himself in her handwriting, the rise and fall of her pen, the individual dots and curls, each of them a communion of sorts: a gentle touch, a warm embrace, a fond farewell.

He comes to the last line of her most recent letter, his eyes now drawn to the words themselves. 'I like you, damn it, and I want you to be happy too. So be brave. Demand more!'

And that's when it happens.

In retrospect, Albert will think of it as an epiphany of angel song, but right now he's almost ashamed of the thought. It's so devious, so underhand, so . . . evil.

He glances at Gloria, hoping for some kind of disapproving stare.

She blinks at him and begins to purr.

It's a sign.

A postman develops an eye for people's habits; the tidal movements that define most people's lives. One of the things that makes Max such a menace in the evenings is his preference for a pint or two after lunch.

And so, for the second time today, Albert finds himself waiting for Max to be predictable, yet this time it's an exhilarating sensation. The hunter and the hunted have swapped roles at last.

Even after he hears Max leave, he waits another ten, fifteen minutes in case he has forgotten something.

Then, with a pounding heart, he does what he's done many times before. He goes to the supermarket.

The cashier doesn't seem surprised that Albert buys six large bottles of bleach. Then again, it's possible she doesn't even notice.

He watches as she pulls them across the scanner, a pudgy young woman moving with all the grace of a badly engineered machine.

'It's getting cold outside,' he says, hopeful that in some small way he can brighten her day, help her find the courage to fight back against the system. For a fleeting moment, she does look him in the eye but, before he can smile, her attention goes back to the slow-moving conveyor-belt, a fitting emblem of her life, an almost Faustian loop of never-ending misery.

Albert thinks about this as he lugs the shopping bags home. Idle chitchat wasn't what the girl needed, and she definitely didn't need to be reminded of the world outside – that was like going to the zoo and telling the penguins that Antarctica was overrated. 'You see, you're much better off trapped in here, sliding about on shit-stained concrete.'

No, what he should have done was squeeze her hand with all the authority of a loving parent and told her very calmly, 'Be brave. Demand more.'

42

CAROL'S DAY IS not going well. It's true that Bob woke up feeling better than he had in several days. No temperature, no aches. This is good news. The bad news is that his cancer has possibly spread and his specialist wants to do more tests as soon as possible.

Carol learns this indirectly, having found him sitting pale and catatonic in the living room, the telephone still gripped tightly in his hand.

'It's okay,' she says, as she sits down beside him. 'We'll deal with this together. You and me.'

There's a long silence before Bob speaks. 'I want to have a party.'

'What?'

'I want to have a party. You know, one final bash.'

'Bob, you make it sound like you're dying.' He visibly shrinks at the mention of that word. 'Sorry. What I mean is, I can think of better times to have a party than this.'

'But if the tests are positive, everything will change. I mean, there'll be chemo and—'

'Bob, you don't need to think about that yet.'

'People will know.'

'It's okay to tell people—'

'No! No one must know.'

'Look, I know how you fee—'

'What – so you have cancer too?'

'Well, no—'

'Then you don't know how I feel, do you? I want a party.'

Carol decides this is not the time for an argument. 'Fine, we'll have a party.'

'Tonight.'

'Bob!'

'I don't have much time left.'

'But it's almost three!'

'What is there to do? We open a few packets of crisps, throw some nuts in a bowl. We just need lots of alcohol, and that's easy.'

'And people, Bob. Most people like to have more than four hours' notice.'

'I doubt Helen would say that.'

'I'm not inviting Helen.' She says it so abruptly, even Bob looks suspicious. 'If I invite Helen, she may figure out what's going on. She's good with stuff like that.'

He appears to believe her. 'Well, all our other friends are sad bastards too. They're bound to be free. And they owe me this.'

'Only if you tell them what's happening.'

'There's nothing to tell.'

'Of course there is – you've got cancer!'

In the stunned silence that follows, Carol tries to imagine how Mother Teresa or Princess Diana would have handled the situation – probably not by shrieking at the cancer patient.

She forces her most gentle, encouraging voice: 'That's what friends are for, Bob. People can't help you through this if you don't let them.'

He seems to consider her words, so that for a moment she believes he's coming around to her point of view. Then he shakes his head. 'No,' he says. 'No one knows.'

Even by the standards of Bob and Carol's social life, turnout for the event is poor. Much as Carol suspected, nobody feels they owe Bob their attendance at a hastily planned party on a mid-week night in an inaccessible part of Croydon. The fact that anyone has come at all would be remarkable, but for the fact that the handful of guests who have made it are all hardcore losers. Bob's mother is here, though she might just as well not be. Solitary by nature, she tends to make stealth attacks on the Pringles before retreating to quiet corners of the room, sometimes wandering away to entirely different parts of the house so she can eat them in private. Carol's parents are also here, though that's no surprise since the alternative is to sit at home hating the sight of each other – and why do that alone when it's much more gratifying to do it in public?

The handful of other people are mostly Bob's colleagues,

not friends so much as orbital debris. 'Do you have any Johnnie Walker?' asks one of them, as he pours himself a large beaker of red wine.

Carol watches as he drinks down the entire cup and tops it back up. 'Sorry, no.'

He holds up the wine bottle, already half gone. 'In that case, I might just keep this with me, if you don't mind.'

Although it's dark outside, another of Bob's colleagues arrives wearing sunglasses, perhaps as a precaution against the paparazzi, or maybe as a distraction from his receding hairline and striking dandruff problem. His face lights up when he sees Carol.

'Hello, you,' he says, with a flourish that's ill suited to the neighbourhood. 'It's been ages.' He gives her a warm hug, his semi-erect penis pressing against her thigh.

Carol struggles to find the right words. In the end, she simply points at the table of food. 'Please, help yourself.'

Watching this roomful of people, she's struck by the urge to lock the house and set fire to the place; to take them all out in one fell swoop. She imagines their screams as they pound at the doors and windows; how they'd slowly be silenced by the thick, acrid smoke, the whole house a fireball, nothing left to suggest the presence of people but the faint scent of charred flesh drifting on the cold night air. It's such a compelling vision, she'd do it right now if only she could. But the logistics . . . A crap party is easy to throw together, but mass murder takes longer to organize.

She watches Bob, the mastermind of tonight's slow-motion tragedy. Despite his enthusiasm for the party, he makes no effort to mingle. Instead he lingers by the drinks, knocking back a bottle of beer in rapid sips that essentially prevent him doing anything but nodding at the other guests. Carol notices he manages a few words whenever his mother sweeps in on one of her table raids, but what they're saying to one another is impossible to tell. They aren't especially close, so it could just as easily be verbal sniping: 'Hope you choke on them, bitch', that sort of thing.

Carol responds the only way she knows how: she busies herself by fussing over the needs of people she'd rather see dead. As she refills a large bowl of pasta salad, she wonders what will become of her now. Bob wanted this party to be a sort of calm before the storm, a moment of celebration before the possible onslaught of his illness, but if this is the silver lining, she doesn't want to see the cloud.

She carries the bowl back through to the dining table. 'There's more salad,' she announces, to no one in particular.

'Have you added any salt to this batch?' says her mother. 'The last lot was very bland.'

Carol watches her mother approach with all the self-assurance of someone on first-name terms with God.

'Despite the food, though, I'm glad to be back. I didn't think we were ever going to be invited again.'

'Well, there you go,' snaps Carol, 'another belief you got wrong.'

She hurries back to the safety of the kitchen, aware that the evening is beginning to derail. From the moment Bob had suggested a party, it was obvious the whole thing would be a train wreck, but Carol had kidded herself she'd somehow be a spectator to the carnage, not one of the passengers.

Deirdre appears in the doorway, strains to push her husband's wheelchair across the shag-pile rug.

'What are you doing?' says Carol.

'Coming to see our daughter. What else would we do in this house?'

This strikes Carol as the most sensible thing her mother has said in years, possibly decades. What else is there to do in this house? Mingle with the chronically damned? Nibble on crap food? You certainly couldn't have a chat with Bob about his cancer.

'I appreciate the thought,' says Carol, 'but this really isn't a good time to talk.'

'Life's not just about you, you know.'

She finally manages to get the wheelchair into the kitchen, instantly making the room feel cramped and claustrophobic.

'What I'm trying to say,' says Carol, 'is that I have a lot on my mind right now.'

'Well, this is the price you pay when you turn away from God.'

'Oh, of course, because you're so happy.'

For a fraction of a second, her father looks as if he wants to run for cover. Stuck there in the middle of a war zone, his facial expression says it all: the opening shots have been fired and there can be no going back now.

'You're one of the unhappiest people I know,' says Carol, her voice rising with every syllable. 'I don't know how that's supposed to be a recommendation for your religious beliefs.'

'The way of truth is one of suffering.'

'You just implied it was one of joy.'

'It's both.'

'Then you can't lose, can you?'

'I'm not the one getting angry.'

'I'm only angry because . . . because you're a nasty little woman who's spent her entire life hiding behind toxic dogma—'

Her mother storms out of the room. Carol follows her into the hallway and shouts after her.

'—and all because you're too scared to just get on with your life and be happy!'

She realizes the other guests are now staring at her, their plastic cups frozen in mid-sip.

Retreating to the kitchen again, she finds her father trying to talk, the words spilling out in an unintelligible gurgle. For all she knows he's trying to say something of immense importance – the kindest, most tender words he will ever speak – but it's lost in a tangle of deadened grey matter, unable to find its way through his injured mind.

Deirdre reappears, steely-faced, her coat thrown loosely over her shoulders. 'We're leaving.' She says it to the back of his head, her eyes not even acknowledging Carol's presence.

As she struggles to drag the wheelchair from the room, Carol and her father stare at one another, two people who understand what it means to be powerless.

43

THIS IS SOMETHING new for Albert. He's been up late before, of course, but only when he's been burdened by regrets and loss. Tonight is different. He sits in the light of a single lamp, the fringes of the room in darkness, and he finds himself enjoying the silence, the anticipation. There's the usual background hum of the city – the sound of South London combusting and going to Hell – but it only heightens the sensation of silence here indoors.

As the hands of the clock tick past midnight, he flashes a smile at Gloria.

'It's time . . .'

Moving stealthily, he props the front door open with a bottle of bleach and steps outside. The air is sharp now, no sunlight to soften winter's approach. Walking in his socks, he carries another bottle of bleach across to Max's plants and begins to pour.

He feels a pang of guilt as the soil in the first pot soaks

up the fluid. Behind him, Max's windows are curtained and in darkness.

'It's nothing personal,' he whispers to the plant. 'You're going to a better place.'

He'd expected to see the plant wilt straight away, but there's no discernible difference. Feeling disappointed – and a little guilty for wanting to see a living thing die – he drains the bottle dry on the second and third pots and then tiptoes back for more.

By the time he's moved on to the third bottle, he's finding the process quite restful. Standing here, gently watering the plants with chlorine, he can see why Max enjoys gardening.

Distracted by the thought, he doesn't notice the lift arrive on his floor. Only as the doors slide open and it casts its light across him does he look up, bleach in mid-flow.

Inside, a couple is kissing with such intensity, it looks more like an act of violence. Albert watches as the girl, much younger than the man, blindly gropes for the right button.

Giving up, she opens her eyes and punches it with a clenched fist. In the split second it takes for the doors to close, she and Albert stare at one another uncomprehendingly: he watering plants with bleach, she with her legs wrapped around a man twice her age. Moments later the doors slide shut and they're gone.

It's one o'clock in the morning and Albert is certain he will never be able to sleep again – will never want to sleep again. Now that he is safely indoors, mission accomplished, the enormity of what he's done is beginning to sink in; the terrifying, thrilling knowledge that it's too late to take any of it back.

He's already thrown the empty bottles of bleach down the rubbish chute, and his dirty socks are hidden at the bottom of the laundry basket. He's impressed how easily it all came to him, this life of covert operations.

It's the kind of news he wants to share.

44

Dear Connie

    I want to thank you for your letters, which I have enjoyed reading. They have brightened my life in unexpected ways.

He hesitates over the words. It isn't true that he's enjoyed reading all of them – the one where she got drunk and abusive, for instance, had ended up in the bin. As for brightening his life in unexpected ways, he worries that might sound a little lecherous, given that she's spent half her time detailing her sexual exploits and fantasies.

    'What would I write if I was her father?' he says to himself.

    This line of reasoning doesn't help, least of all because she probably wouldn't have written any of those things to her father, and if she had she'd be getting a good slap, not a letter of thanks.

    Deciding it's better simply to go with the flow, he continues.

Your last letter in particular inspired me. I think I'd become a frightened old man. I'm still an old man, but your words have helped me feel braver. I want to thank you for that.

When I was in the army

He crosses the line out, stares at it, then screws the whole sheet into a ball.

Gloria watches as, moments later, he unfolds it and flattens it out on the table.

'It'll do for shopping lists, won't it? Waste not, want not.'

He puts the crumpled sheet to one side and takes a new one.

Dear Connie

I don't want to be the kind of old man who talks about the war, so I won't. To be honest, I'm not really old enough to talk about the war. I was born in 1946, almost nine months to the day after the war ended. No guessing how my parents celebrated that victory.

He stops writing, startled by his ability to be that frank. 'I'm getting as bad as her.' Yet it feels good, this freedom to talk as he wouldn't dare talk to anyone else.

Even though I'm not old enough, I think it's fair to say I have more in common with the war years than with today's world. Life was different back then. You probably think I sound like a lunatic, talking fondly about wartime. That's the problem, I suppose. Either the world has gone mad or I have.

I want you to know that your letters have made an incredible difference to a lonely old man. Some of them have been a little racy for my tastes, but it's who we are in our hearts that matters, not the things we've done.

He lingers over that paragraph too. It sounds wise and fatherly, which is the intention. It also makes him feel better about having just killed Max's entire garden. With a sense of absolution already setting in, he continues writing.

I didn't know I was lonely until I got your letters. You might think it's strange for someone to be grateful for that, but it woke me up. It woke me up to what I'd become. You see, my wife died almost forty years ago and a part of me died with her.

His eyes begin to well, but still he keeps writing.

When you lose someone you love

The first tear falls to the page. He stops writing and clumsily wipes his face with the back of his hand.

'Pull yourself together, Albert.'

He glances at Gloria, ashamed that she's seen him cry. 'Don't worry, I'm fine now.'

In a strange way, hearing that you don't love your husband has reminded me how much I loved my wife. In that respect, we share a bond, don't you think? You've never had that kind of marriage, and I lost mine. Two different paths have brought us to the same place.

When she was alive, I promised my wife I would never spend a night away, and I keep that promise even now. I've kept her pillow and I hold it close every night.

She died on that pillow

The tears come again, faster and heavier now. This time, he keeps writing even as they fall to the page and start to smudge the ink.

and it was without warning, that was the thing. She'd never been sick, or not to speak of anyway. She was so young and full of life, so many things we wanted to do together. You see, we were in love, so very, very in love. Then she was gone, just like that. Her heart stopped beating while she slept. The doctor told me it was a peaceful death and I think he's right. She was there, in my arms, you see. I would have known if she was in pain. I would have known.

So I have the pillow and some of her clothes, just a few things, but I don't like to look at them these days. It doesn't help, you see. It doesn't bring her back, it just takes me back. Takes me a back to a time when

I failed her. When she was in my arms and I couldn't save her, couldn't keep her with me. I live with that regret. I have done for the last forty years. I tell myself there was nothing I could have done, but I don't know that, do you understand? I will never know for sure.

And there's one thing I'm so ashamed of—

He gasps, barely even able to write the words.

—I can't remember the sound of her voice. The woman I loved more than life itself and I can't remember what she sounded like. Only that her voice made me happy every time I heard it.

45

IT WOULD BE wrong to say the party went downhill after Carol's parents left: the event had been in freefall long before that. Their angry departure was really the moment of impact, when the inertia of sad, sorry lives crashed headlong into reality. From that moment on, the remaining guests seemed almost embarrassed to be there – as if they at last understood the tragedy of their own lives by looking at the people around them – and one by one they drifted away.

To his credit, Bob seemed unfazed by the drama, possibly even found some comfort in the thought that external reality was no better than his own inner chaos.

He drifted off to bed soon after the final guest left, too drunk to do anything else, so Carol has spent the rest of the evening alone.

Even now, as time crosses that indeterminate line between very late and very early, she doesn't want to sleep, doesn't want to do anything that might hasten the arrival of yet another day. Better just to stay downstairs in a silent house surrounded by dirty plates and wine-stained plastic cups.

She goes looking for her laptop, a present from Bob last Christmas. It was supposed to bring her roaring into the twenty-first century, connecting her with long-lost friends and giving her access to email at all times, but it hasn't worked out that way. She's lost touch with old friends for good reason, and what emails is she supposed to be getting? Her relationship with Bob and Sophie is dysfunctional, but at least they still talk to one another. Helen would sooner send smoke signals than an email, so who else is there? Much like her presence in real-life, Mandy would only be good for spam, and Carol's colleagues would just abuse the system to make themselves feel more valuable, using evenings and weekends to talk about work that barely even matters during business hours.

As far as Bob is concerned, the gift was a mistake, but that isn't entirely true. For Carol, it has become a repository, a place for saving memories away from prying eyes. Naturally, this isn't something she's told Bob, so the computer has inadvertently become a symbol of the distance between them – not only that he doesn't understand her, but that he doesn't really know her either.

As the screen flickers into life, she feels a pang of guilt. She's about to revisit a memory best left in the past, but she can't stop now . . .

46

I still have his picture. Have I ever mentioned that? I shouldn't, I know, but there you go. In my defence, I don't look at it very often. My husband doesn't know, of course. It's ironic, really, that I use the computer he gave me to store a picture of the man I cheated on him with. Though 'cheated' is the wrong word, don't you think? 'Cheated' implies I was stringing my husband along at the same time, which isn't true. I wasn't telling him I loved him every day. I wasn't talking about our future together. We were simply married, raising our child. My heart was always with Richard.

She stops writing, stares at Richard's picture on screen. It isn't a particularly good photo, but it's all she has from those days, and it's enough. He still looks as young and fresh as he was that first time, his skin taut and firm beneath her fingers, between her legs.

I need to let go of the past, but there's a big part of me that prefers the past to now. It wasn't just Richard, it was me too: life seemed so full of promise back then – I still believed in possibilities and dreams and happy endings. Maybe it's not Richard I miss at all, but me.

And then I look into his eyes and I know what I really miss is us.

She's interrupted by the sound of car doors slamming out on the street. Moments later, drunken, high-pitched laughter.

Carol gently pulls back the curtains to find her neighbours with the flagpole staggering about their garden in party hats.

She watches as the wife struggles to take off her bra, a cigarette hanging loosely from her lips. While she twists and contorts, her husband lowers the flag, pausing every few seconds to take another swig from a bottle of sparkling wine.

Steadying herself against the sheer bulk of their expensive four-wheel drive, the wife pulls her bra free. She snatches the bottle of wine and drinks thirstily while her husband swaps the flag for the bra and starts to hoist.

In the absence of a stiff wind, it isn't apparent that the limp and lacy rag dangling at the top of the flagpole is a bra. For the couple, however, it's evidently the climax of the evening. They collapse into fits of laughter, their knees buckling beneath them.

Carol frowns at their hilarity – at this exact moment, she can imagine at least two places she'd like to stick the flagpole

– and yet who wouldn't be jealous of a married couple having so much fun? If this is what they could make of a cold mid-week night in Croydon, what would they be like on holiday? And who was Carol by contrast? The unhappy housewife spying on her neighbours in the dead of night.

'I've become my mother,' she mutters to herself.

Turning away from the window, she makes a mental note never to judge her neighbours again. Let them drive pretentious cars and fill their gardens with flagpoles. Is any of that worse than her own decisions in life?

Needing more alcohol to soften the introspection, she wanders into the kitchen and pours herself a large glass of wine.

'There are children dying in Africa,' she says to herself. 'It would be shameful to waste it.' Glass in hand, she turns to find Sophie watching her. 'Shit,' she cries, so startled she almost spills her drink. 'I didn't hear you come in.'

'I thought everyone would be asleep.' There's a hint of criticism in her voice, as though Carol's wakefulness is indicative of some deeper pathology.

'We had a party.'

'Why?'

Carol struggles over an appropriate response, alcohol making it harder to lie. 'Well, why not? It was a chance to catch up with old friends.'

Sophie is obviously dissatisfied with the answer. As she wanders out of sight, Carol chugs her glass of wine and pours another, pausing between mouthfuls to call through the wall, 'What were you doing tonight?'

'Helping Rebecca with her physics.'

Naturally, thinks Carol. What else would a seventeen-year-old girl be doing at three in the morning?

For a moment she wonders how it would be if Sophie had come home tearful and overwrought with tales of sex gone wrong – a sordid drunken encounter, perhaps even several, that had left her worrying about STDs and pregnancy. For the first time in years, Carol would actually feel she had something to share.

'Who's this?' says Sophie.

Carol rushes from the kitchen to find Sophie peering at the computer screen, her expression a mixture of interest and suspicion.

'It's no one, just an old friend.'

'How "old"?'

'Oh, a year or two after university. His name's Richard.' Hearing herself say it breathes new life into the memory, brings a smile to her face. 'We worked together years ago. He left after a few months, but we . . . we kept in touch.'

It feels like such a release, this veiled honesty, she wants to say more, much more. She imagines explaining how Sophie even met him once, on a day so happy and perfect it seemed like nothing in life would ever be wrong again.

She glances at the pad of writing paper, thankfully turned face down.

'I was just writing him a letter—'

'Isn't that what the computer's for?'

'Well, I'm a bit backward, I'm afraid.'

At last, she's said something credible.

With a final look at the picture, Sophie heads for bed, climbing the stairs with all the stealth of a born predator.

My daughter has just seen his picture. In terms of Things a Mother Shouldn't Do, that seems a bit like giving her a puff on my crack pipe. Not that I smoke crack, by the way, though you'd be forgiven for assuming I do. It would certainly account for a lot.

She stood there looking at my most intimate secret. It could have been the ultimate mother-daughter moment. I think I even wanted it to be. But then the moment was gone.

Being rational, she probably wouldn't want to know that I fell in love with that man. How we fucked with all the passion of true soul-mates. Though maybe she'd be interested to hear why I stayed with her father. She'd certainly take some satisfaction in hearing I've regretted it ever since. She likes cataloguing my mistakes.

There's so much else I could tell you about the evening . . . a catastrophic party (at least I had a legitimate excuse to drink more than usual tonight) . . . and now the people across the street have hoisted a bra on their flagpole. I'm not sure which is more shocking, that there's underwear flying at full mast opposite my house or that there's a flagpole. I mean, a FLAGPOLE???? Who puts a flagpole in their garden? If we were at war I might understand it, but even then, isn't a flagpole the kind of thing invading armies and low-flying bombers use as a landmark? I should probably say here that it's not normally used for underwear. On most days, a Union Jack flutters in the breeze, which is supposed to make us all feel patriotic. Patriotism isn't what I'm feeling about the flagpole right now, though maybe I'll begin feeling more English once I see the bloody thing fall on their car.

So it's official: our cul-de-sac (Christ, I hate that word) has sunk to new lows.

Of course, the much more pertinent question is, what am I doing living here? I'm sure there's a moral in there somewhere . . .

From Hell.

C.

47

ALBERT IS STILL padding about the flat in his dressing-gown when Max's first anguished cry echoes across the estate.

He pulls on some clothes and rushes outside to find Max staring at his garden, his eyes wet and puffy with tears.

'Look what the bastards did to my plants.' He gestures at the rows of pots, each of them miniature killing fields, a mass grave of withered stems and poisoned soil. 'They put enough bleach on them to kill us all. Even that much water would have done it, but bleach . . .'

He wipes away a tear, avoids eye contact with Albert.

'Those plants, they were all I had.'

Albert wants to point out this isn't entirely true. He still has a wife, and a big-screen television – he saw that being delivered a few months ago – not to mention an extensive collection of Engelbert Humperdinck albums that he seems quite fond of. Compared to Albert, Max has plenty; that's always been the problem.

Yet that isn't the Max standing beside him now. This Max

is a real human being, vulnerable and emotional, almost endearing in his disconsolation.

Albert pats him on the shoulder, something he's never imagined doing. He's often dreamed of punching Max, pushing him over the parapet, even running him through with a Samurai sword, but comforting him, never.

'I can help you put a new garden together,' he says. 'Between the two of us, we'll have it done in no time.'

Max seems to consider the offer, his tears now mere snuffles. He blows his nose loudly.

'And why the fuck would I want your help? If it's not enough I've got those – those sneaky scumbags wrecking everything.' He picks up one of the flowerpots and throws it from the walkway, shouting across the estate as he does so, 'You fucking bastards!'

His voice echoes over the rooftops as the pot arcs through the air and crashes to earth six floors below. He picks up another and lobs that too.

'You hear me?' he yells again. 'You're fucking bastards, the lot of you!'

He stoops to pick up another.

'I don't think you should be doing that, Max.'

'Piss off!'

He chucks the pot over the edge, managing another two before it even hits the ground.

Aware that there's nothing else he can do, Albert retreats to his flat. Even with the front door closed, the air is thick with the sound of Max's cries and the distant explosions of terracotta on concrete.

'Fuck you all, you hear me? When I find out who did this, I'm going to fucking kill them!'

48

By the time Carol wakes up, the Union Jack is back on the flagpole as if nothing had happened. She stares at it from her bedroom window, unable to shake the thought that she only imagined the bra, imagined everything from the night before. Her hangover just adds to the sensation that she's losing her grip on reality.

The events of the night – her mother storming off, her daughter seeing Richard, her husband sleeping peacefully even as his body begins to self-destruct – these feel more like scenes from a movie than her own life. And how would that kind of movie end? she wonders. A happy ending doesn't seem very likely, not this late in the film. It's more probable that the world as they know it is moving towards some tragic inevitability. A comet strike would be too random, too much of a coincidence, but a sinkhole, perhaps – yes, that's it. A large sinkhole is quietly carving out the ground beneath their feet, so even as they battle on in their daily lives – arguing and lying and secretly resenting one another – the world as they know it is literally disappearing; the seconds counting down until the earth swallows them all, the whole cul-de-sac gone. The movie's final scene will last just long enough for the deafening roar to fade to a poignant beat of pure silence – the kind of purity that never existed in their daily lives – and then the end credits will begin to roll.

From the eyrie of Carol's bedroom window, it doesn't just seem plausible, it feels entirely probable that her world will soon disappear, that something deep down, out of sight, is threatening to destroy everything.

She hears the dull thud of the front door slamming. Moments later, Sophie walks away from the house, her bag heavy with books she'll doubtless have memorized by the end of the day.

The car is still in the driveway, which can only mean Bob is downstairs eating or playing World of Warcraft, or more likely doing both simultaneously.

He'll be leaving soon for more tests – heading off to the hospital alone yet again – though Carol tries to remind herself these aren't like animal tests: the hospital staff won't be rubbing shampoo in his eyes or injecting him with weed-killer. Instead they'll be fussing over him and giving him the kind of attention he's craved for years. By getting cancer, his inner hypochondriac has finally hit the jackpot. There must be some satisfaction in that.

Bob is so engrossed in his computer, he barely notices Carol enter the living room, her bed-head and ageing dressing-gown suggesting she doesn't care about anything any longer.

'How long have you been up?' she says, as she searches the room for her mobile phone.

'An hour or two.' He doesn't look at her as he speaks, his full attention on the computer. 'I thought I'd let you sleep.'

Carol scrolls through her missed calls. Two from Helen – she won't be returning those anytime soon – and one from her mother. It's obvious why *she* called. Not to apologize, of course, not even to discuss it, but rather to pretend it never happened; to overlay the memory with the usual inane chitchat. That's her timeworn habit, of burying pain, secretly storing it up as ammunition for future use. In many ways that's the whole problem with their relationship: the weapons cache that is their shared history has made it feel less like a familial bond than a hostage situation, so that to sit in the same room as Deirdre is to accept that at any moment everyone may die.

'Not going to work today?' says Bob.

'God, I hadn't even thought of that.' She glances down at her dressing-gown as though it's a physical condition rather than a piece of clothing. 'I'll just call in sick.'

'Everything's falling apart, isn't it?' He doesn't sound troubled by the statement, doesn't even seem aware of his profundity. 'Everything our life used to be, it's all gone, just like that.'

DEATH

49

WITH LESS THAN a week to go before his retirement, Albert knows only one thing: he has to find Connie. The odds are stacked against him, but the alternative is to spend the rest of his life poring over five letters in an old biscuit tin. There's Gloria to occupy him, but being realistic she doesn't have that many years left. And once her plaster comes off, who's to say she won't take another leap from the window? As much as Albert loves her, she won't be much company dead.

It's Connie who's helped him see that it's okay to want more from life, and the first thing he wants is her.

He knows she posted the letters in Croydon. Assuming that she lives there too – and her letters contain enough snide references about the place to suggest she does – that already reduces the odds of finding her from one-in-tens-of-million to . . . well, a lot less.

Mickey ambles in with a Get Well Soon card.

'Want to sign this?' he says. 'It's for Chris.'

'What's wrong with him?'

'Broke his leg skateboarding.'

Albert opens it up and scribbles a message: 'Serves you right, you daft bugger.'

'Have you heard about your surprise party next week? Indian food,' says Mickey with a grimace. 'I fucking hate Indian!'

'Nobody asked me if I like Indian.'

'Well, they wouldn't, would they? It's a surprise. Anyway, it's Darren's favourite restaurant.'

'But it's my party.'

'And he's the boss. I mean, it's a perk, isn't it? Like a company car, but a curry.' He looks at the card and sighs. 'I ought to get going. Gary needs to sign this, though the dense bastard probably doesn't know how. He spends a bit too much time wanking, that's his problem.' He pauses, obviously considering the subject from a new angle. 'What's it like when you get old? Do you still play with yourself much?'

Albert decides to ignore him. 'Actually, I've got a question for you. How many people do you think live in Croydon?'

This isn't the right sort of thing to ask Mickey, Albert's aware of that. By all means ask if there are aliens in London's sewers or which TV celebrities like to be fist-fucked. Mickey considers himself an authority on subjects like this – is probably disappointed that CNN and the BBC haven't beaten a path to his door – but a straightforward question with a quantifiable answer, that's a different matter.

'I don't know,' he says, after a long pause. 'Maybe twenty million?'

Albert realizes he may as well have asked for the population of Calcutta, or the whereabouts of Atlantis. 'I think you should go and find Gary,' he says.

'Why? Do you think he'd know?'

'For the card.'

'Oh, yeah . . .' He wanders from the room, still staring at the card as if he can't remember what he's supposed to be doing with it.

Working on the basis that Mickey knows absolutely nothing, Albert decides the population of Croydon is probably a few hundred thousand, definitely less than half a million. And so the haystack grows smaller by the minute. 'At this rate I'll find her in no time.'

'What was that, Albert?'

He turns to see Darren rushing in with his usual pomp and swagger.

'Nothing,' says Albert. 'Just talking to myself.'

Darren seems unsurprised – was possibly even expecting it.

'What happened yesterday?' he says. 'Don't say I have to dock your pay so close to retirement . . .'

'I was here as usual.' He holds Darren's gaze, steady, unruffled. 'I was probably just in the toilet.'

'I came by three or four times.'

'That's the trouble with getting older. It all loosens up, takes on a mind of its own.'

He watches Darren cringe.

'There are times,' he continues, 'when it comes out like slurry for days and d—'

'Yeah, that's fine, Albert. You can spare me the details.' He glances at his watch. 'Well, if everything's in order—'

'You have meetings.'

Darren looks floored, unaccustomed to Albert acting like this.

'Just so you know,' he says, 'we're thinking of having a small do on your last day. Nothing much, you understand, what with budget cuts and all. A pot of tea, maybe some sandwiches and cake.' He smiles, clearly enjoying the subterfuge. 'I just want to make sure you're okay with that.'

'Tea and cake sound perfect. To be honest, anything else gives me terrible wind.'

Darren smiles stiffly, doubtless imagining the many ways in which Albert could ruin his big night out. 'Well, that's settled then, isn't it?'

Albert begins his search on Saturday. He doesn't have much to go on, but Connie has made several references to living on an estate. She seems to have a pretty low opinion of it, but to Albert's mind it sounds quite posh. Never mind the flagpoles, the fact that people have somewhere to put them already suggests they're doing okay. And in as much as they don't get nicked during the night, it has to be a nicer area than his own.

After making his way to Croydon, it takes him a while to find an appropriate estate agent, each of them furtively assessed while he pretends to view properties in the window. As far as he can tell, his final choice is ideal: the only person working in there is a middle-aged woman with a desperate look about her, clearly open to any kind of distraction, even someone like Albert.

As he steps inside, he uses the cheeriest voice he can muster. 'Hello, I, er, I want to buy a house.'

The woman had sat up when he first opened the door, perhaps preparing to offer directions to a confused pensioner, but now she looks bewildered. 'Are you selling your current house too?' she says.

'No, no, I just want to buy one. Do you offer that service?'

'So you've already sold your house?' She's staring at his Royal Mail coat. 'This will be a cash purchase?'

'Well, no . . . I was thinking I may get a mortgage.' He gives her a smile and gestures at the logo on his coat. 'As you can see, I'm gainfully employed.'

Whether she feels sorry for him or simply wants a distraction, she gives him a big smile. 'Do you have an area in mind?'

'I was thinking of a nice estate. The kind that's popular with families.'

Her name is Marjorie and she doesn't enjoy being an estate agent.

'I thought I'd be selling houses every week,' she says, with a sigh. 'I thought it'd be easy money.'

Easy money. Albert has never used that expression. It sounds profligate, reckless, the twin brother of easy debt. Yet Marjorie doesn't seem profligate and reckless. There's none of the boastful showiness that Albert associates with that kind of person. Instead she just looks worn at the edges, like an old carpet that's past its prime, the kind of thing that probably looked nice twenty years ago, before everyone started running across it in golf shoes and football boots, before the cat puked on it and the dog began marking its territory.

'To be honest, it's nice just to get out for a while,' she says, as she locks up the shop and lights a cigarette. 'Maybe if I could smoke at work, it might be easier. But, of course, there's a law against that.' She takes a long, indignant drag on her cigarette. 'It's not as if I'm the only estate agent in town. If people don't like nicotine, they can go somewhere else. That could have been my thing, you know. I could have been the woman who helps smokers find new homes. God knows, you need some way of standing out in this market. It's like swimming with piranhas, everyone fighting over the odd tadpole here and there.'

'Business not going well, then?'

Marjorie snorts and takes another long drag, as if her only option now is to try to die young.

'My timing was awful, of course. I opened the office just as everything crashed. You hear all those wankers on television saying a recession is a wonderful time to buy, but buy what? Who's going to sell when prices have gone through the floor?'

She herds Albert towards a small car park. On the far side, a beaten-up Astra and a Range Rover sit side by side.

'Guess which is mine.'

'Well, I'm hoping it's that one,' says Albert, pointing to the Astra. 'I don't think I could get in the other one without a stepladder.'

'True, but you might need a winch to get out of mine.' She rushes ahead of him and starts tossing clothes and empty beer cans from the front passenger seat. 'Despite how it looks, I don't live in my car. Not yet, anyway.'

Albert has never had a car, but even to his untrained ear it sounds as if Marjorie's Astra will soon be fit for nothing but sleeping in. The engine reminds him of the noise lawnmowers make when stones get stuck in the blades, and the entire car rattles as if it's held together by luck rather than engineering. Despite this, Marjorie drives it like a defensive weapon, manoeuvring around every other car on the road as though she's in a fight to the death. She doesn't talk as she drives, doesn't even seem to be aware of Albert's presence any more; she simply stares at the road ahead, her face writ large with all the focus of a kamikaze pilot.

She starts to speak again only as they pull into a sprawling housing estate. 'Look at this place,' she says, with disgust. 'It's like Legoland. And for this, you get saddled with a massive mortgage and a lifetime of misery.'

If this is her standard sales pitch, thinks Albert, it's no wonder business is slow. To his eye, the houses actually look quite nice; snug rather than small. Every front door is painted a bright, cheerful colour, and none of them hide behind the heavy metal grilles of his own estate.

Marjorie brakes sharply, bracing herself against the steering-wheel as the car lurches to a halt in front of a small terraced house. 'This is the one,' she says.

Albert gazes up at its windows, bare and forlorn compared to the neighbours on either side. Left alone like this, it looks sad and incomplete – a state that Albert can relate to.

'It's lovely, isn't it?' he says, as much to himself as Marjorie.

'Do you mind letting yourself in? I need another fag. And, of course, the nicotine Nazis won't let me do that inside.'

She hands him a key and shoos him from the car. Seconds later she's disappearing in a cloud of Benson & Hedges while Albert crosses the small front garden – big enough for a deckchair and a portable radio, everything a man needs – and slips the key into the lock. With barely a turn, the door swings open on well-oiled hinges. Already feeling the kind of love that most people only experience for new-born grandchildren, he steps inside, eyes wide with the wonder of it all.

Although the day is supposed to be about Connie, he can't think of her right now, not when he's looking at the kind of kitchen his wife would have loved. Bigger than his own and fitted with matching cabinets, it's the nicest kitchen he's ever seen. 'I just wish I could have given it to you,' he says softly. 'They never had this sort of thing back in our day, did they?'

He peers inside the refrigerator, a cavernous white space. 'We would've had to breed like rabbits to need something this big. Not that you'd have said no, you saucy girl!'

He wanders into the living room, where french windows look out on a small garden, its square of grass enclosed on three sides by empty flowerbeds and a high wooden fence. 'Would you look at that?' he says, in unabashed awe. 'We could grow half our vegetables out there and still have room for your roses. That's what it was, wasn't it? Roses round the doorway. And maybe a little Albert playing with his tin soldiers . . .'

He can imagine her swooning over the garden – if she hadn't already passed out from excitement in the kitchen – and the thought makes her feel somehow present. If he could just stand here for ever and hold this moment, they'd never have to be apart again.

Marjorie enters the room, cutting through the stillness with a tubercular cough. 'Bloody cigarettes,' she wheezes. 'I should give up, but what would I have left then?' She thumps her chest a few times and appears to swallow some loose phlegm. 'So, what do you think of the house?'

'It's gorgeous.'

'Well, that's what we like to hear. The price is good too. Though no one will be saying that in a year's time when it's worth thirty per cent less. Have you taken a look upstairs?'

'I don't think that'll be necessary.'

'I thought you liked it?'

'I do, but . . . I've not been entirely honest with you. I'm not really in a position to move.'

As Marjorie has looked disappointed all morning, possibly even most of her life, there's no discernible reaction. 'Well, I can't say I blame you,' she says, with a sigh. 'Who in their right mind wants anything to do with property these days? It's nothing but a one-way ticket to misery.' She fishes her car keys from her handbag. 'How about I run you back into town?'

'There's no need,' he says, a little too quickly. He's no statistician, but having survived the journey out, it seems unlikely they'll get back in one piece too. 'I was thinking I might wander around a bit, take a look at the neighbourhood.'

'What's there to look at? It's just lots of crappy little houses full of depressed people.' She waits, obviously expecting him to come to his senses. 'God,' she says, 'you really are serious. Well, I'd offer to join you, but I should get back to the shop. You never know when someone might wander in with a blank cheque! Though they could wander in with a gun for all I care. Might do me a favour if someone just came in and shot me in the head.'

She falls silent, evidently savouring the prospect.

'It was nice to meet you,' says Albert.

'Oh,' she replies, startled. 'Likewise. And look me up if you change your mind about the house. Dead or alive, I'll be in the office.'

Back out on the pavement, Albert waits while Marjorie straps herself into the car and fires up the engine. From out here, it sounds as though the vehicle will sooner explode than move. Albert can imagine them both being vaporized in a fireball of unleaded petrol, nothing left to indicate their fate except a large, smouldering crater.

With a loud crunch of the clutch, she's suddenly off. He thinks he sees her wave goodbye as she shoots away, but it could just as easily have been the G-force of her acceleration, one hand torn free of the steering-wheel as the car surged forward.

A few seconds later, she's disappeared from view and Albert finds himself alone again.

*

He'd imagined it would be easy finding Connie's house. He didn't necessarily expect her to be at home, and he definitely hadn't figured out what to say if she was, but his instincts told him that finding the house itself would be strangely effortless, almost fated. After all, the gods had been working in his favour when he got her first letter; they surely wouldn't let him down now.

He was wrong. Having spent four or five hours walking streets that all looked the same, the only thing he knows for sure is that his shoes are useless. The soles feel so thin and flimsy, he may as well be walking barefoot, and the back of one shoe has rubbed his heel into a patchwork of oozing blisters. The discomfort was easy to bear while he believed Connie's house was waiting around the next corner or the corner after that, but as hope slowly began to fade the pain became worse and the cold wind started to bite through him.

By the time he limps into the lift at home, he's one of the walking wounded, as damaged emotionally as physically. He's certainly ill prepared for what comes into view as the lift doors creak open on his floor: Max has replaced his entire garden. Row upon row of bright flowers now wave in the wind, their colours almost neon in the gloaming.

It's only as Albert hobbles closer that he realizes they're all fake. Pot after pot of plastic flowers, each of them crudely glued down so they can never be moved again.

They're so striking in their artifice, Albert finds himself stopping to take a closer look. He's heard that some plastic flowers are now so lifelike, people can't tell the difference. If that's true, they're not the kind of flowers Max has bought.

His are a crude approximation of nature, the sort of thing that speaks of a Dickensian factory in a remote, blighted corner of China, the workers too blinded and crippled by toxic chemicals to realize they're creating aberrations.

He'd expected Max to come charging out by now, shooing him away in the usual torrent of abuse, but instead there's nothing. The curtains are tightly drawn shut, and the only sound is the rustle of plastic flowers moving in the wind.

50

On a cold, dark, wet night in Croydon, the last thing Carol expects is to make peace with her mother – and yet here's Deirdre, asking Carol to forgive her.

'I've been a bad mother.'

'No, no, that's not true,' replies Carol. She doesn't mean this, of course, but she feels the need to say something to take the edge off her mother's rush of self-awareness. 'I mean, it must have been hard . . . with Dad and all . . .'

'But that was no excuse, I can see that now.' She smiles, her face radiant. She looks younger and more alive than Carol has ever seen her before. 'What you said was right. I have been scared. My entire life, I've been too frightened to really live. Too frightened to love.' Carol feels her pulse quicken as Deirdre sits down beside her, so close she can feel her breath. 'I'm worried I taught you to be scared too.'

'No, I . . . I don't know. I'm fine.'

'I want you to know, I'm so proud of the woman you've become.'

'I haven't really become anything.'

'But you have, don't you see?'

She leans in closer and Carol knows what's coming. She begins to cry as her mother hugs her, holding her so close, she can feel the warmth of her body, the beat of her heart.

'I love you so much, Carol. I want you to know that. I will always love you.'

Carol gasps through her tears, clings to her now, wanting never to let go. 'And I . . . and I love—'

She sits bolt upright in bed, breathless, her cheeks wet.

Confused, she looks around for her mother – expects her to reappear at the bedside and pick up where they left off. But, no, the room is dark and quiet, Bob dozing peacefully beside her, the sound of rain pattering against the window.

Then the thought comes burning through her synapses, so compelling she finds herself saying it aloud.

'My God, she's dead! She's dead.'

Bob mumbles in his sleep. As his groans fade back into silence, Carol carefully slips out of bed and tiptoes from the room.

Downstairs, she gropes for her telephone in the dark; she doesn't want to turn the light on yet, doesn't want anything to make the moment feel more real than it does already.

She dials and waits for the call to connect, every second feeling like an eternity.

Finally—

Engaged.

Her father must have knocked the phone off the hook again, is maybe even panicking now that Deirdre is sprawled on the floor, a rigid corpse in Marks & Spencer nightwear.

Without hesitating, Carol pulls a coat over her nightgown and runs out to the car, her mind so busy she's not even aware of the rain.

It's only when she sees herself in the rear-view mirror that she realizes how wet she is. Her hair sticks to her scalp like melted plastic, and every inch of her face looks damp to the touch.

She drives fast through the empty, rain-slicked streets. It feels right that she's the only car on the road, as though the entire town has been created specifically for this moment in her life, an elaborate backdrop all her own.

In years to come she knows she'll remember these details, the way the car sounds on the wet streets, how her every breath is visible in the cold air. And through it all, the overwhelming sense of travelling through a desolate place, an entire city stripped of life and movement.

In the rush to get to her parents' house, she hadn't thought what she'd do when she arrived. Although her mother is dead and her father is a cripple, she still rings the doorbell, instinctively slipping back into the role of anxious child standing at the gates of Hell. It's only as she listens to the bell echo through the darkened house that she remembers times have changed. She's in charge now. Her father is depending on her.

She runs to the car and rummages in the boot for Bob's toolbox. She quickly finds a thick-set wrench, heavy and solid in her hands. She carries it back to the house, the rain dripping from her hair, running into her eyes, finding its way between her toes.

With no glass to smash in the front door, she has no choice but to wade through a flowerbed to the living-room window. Seeing her reflection in the glass, she's struck by the irony that she spent her entire childhood trying to escape from this house, and now here she is trying to break in.

She watches as her reflection raises the wrench high above her head, holding it there in a moment of pure potential, and then brings it crashing down through the window.

She hadn't expected it to make so much noise, an ear-splitting cascade of glass that seems to break a million times over. Within seconds, lights are coming on in nearby houses. More alarmingly, lights are coming on in her parents' house too.

It's the sound of footsteps on the stairs that makes Carol most nervous. Moments later, the living-room light comes on and Deirdre enters the room, her hair in curlers and her unmade-up face looking ten years older.

They stare at one another, the floor between them covered with sparkling fragments of glass.

'I thought you were dead,' says Carol.

'Of course you did. Why else would you be smashing the window at three in the morning? And trampling the flowerbeds.'

Carol looks down at the muddy tangle of broken stems beneath her feet.

'Your father's probably had another stroke with all the stress.'

'Is he awake too?'

'Carol, half of Croydon is awake now.' She glances out at the street and tightens her dressing-gown. 'Thanks to you, the neighbours are also watching our every move.'

Carol feels the weight of the wrench in her hand and realizes this probably looks quite bad, an intruder with a blunt metal object attacking an old woman's house in the dead of night. She turns and gives a cheery wave to the onlookers, but they just stare back; alarmed, fascinated.

'I think it's better if you just go home,' says Deirdre. 'Though how we're supposed to sleep now that the window's gone . . .'

'I think the rain is beginning to ease up.'

'And what of the drunken louts and murderers wandering the streets?'

'Then let me—'

'No, thank you. I'll do it myself. It will give me something else to do in my life of leisure. Though I'll be sending you a bill for the repairs.'

'Of course.'

Carol stands there, desperately wanting the moment to be something other than this. Can't they laugh about it? Can't they give thanks that death hasn't come between them after all? It's easy to imagine how different things could be – mother and daughter laughing over a cup of tea, over the monumental task of clearing it all up – she just doesn't know how to make it happen. It's a promised land of love and intimacy that she can see but not reach.

Knowing she'll cry if she stays any longer, she turns to leave.

'Before you go,' says Deirdre, 'I do have one question. Why did you think I'd died?'

'I had a dream.'

Deirdre stares at her. 'Well, very nice, I must say. Rushing over here when you think I'm gone. If only you showed the same enthusiasm when you know I'm alive.'

Unable to respond, Carol goes back to her car, suddenly aware of how cold and wet she really is. Even as she starts the engine, she can see Deirdre in the living room, still watching her.

She should go home, she knows that, but the thought of going back to Bob feels as impossible as staying here. She pulls away, still not sure where she's going, only that she has to keep on the move.

51

He shouldn't have come back, he knows that. His feet hurt, and although the rain has stopped, a stiff wind is scouring the streets. This is no weather for anyone to be outdoors, let alone at his age, and yet what's the alternative? He can feel time slipping away, each passing day bringing him closer to the edge of a precipice. Finding Connie means the difference between tumbling over the edge and trying to fly.

He stops for a cup of tea in an empty cafeteria. He prefers them empty; has always lacked the courage to walk into a crowded café alone. Unfortunately, the empty ones are normally empty for a reason. In his time he's experienced it all: cold tea, sticky tables, rude service, odd smells. On this occasion he's served by a woman who obviously hates life. Not just her own, but everybody's. It's apparent as soon as he enters – a brooding malevolence that drains all the joy from the air. He wants to leave, but she's already staring at him from behind the till and it seems rude to just turn around.

Looking on the bright side, at least his cup of overpriced,

lukewarm dishwater has bought him ten minutes of relative warmth.

He sits in the window and watches the pained expressions on people's faces as they struggle against the wind, occasional rubbish blowing through the streets. There's a dereliction to the scene that reminds him of news reports from war zones: the displaced struggling with what few possessions they still have. Croydon even offers a backdrop that makes the fantasy seem believable. These aren't just passers-by, they're the unlucky and the damned, the ones who couldn't get out of town on the last helicopter, and now here they are, fighting their way through a cityscape ideally suited to heavy artillery fire and mortar rounds.

The woman appears beside him, startling him from his thoughts. 'Will there be anything else?' she says.

'Oh . . . no, thank you.'

She snatches away his empty teacup. 'Then I imagine you'll be leaving now.'

Deciding it's best not to antagonize a woman with access to knives, Albert pulls on his coat and heads for the door.

As he steps out into the cold wind, it strikes him as odd that he's looking for something he doesn't even know how to find, a task that isn't frustrating so much as aimless.

Choosing to turn left, if only so he doesn't have the wind blowing in his face, he realizes that he, too, has become one of the dispossessed, a refugee fleeing the abyss of an uncertain future . . .

52

'SO YOU JUST drove up and down the same stretch of the M25?'. says Helen. 'For three hours?'

'It's quiet at that time of night.'

'That's not really the point. Your angst now has a carbon footprint the size of Wales.'

Perhaps realizing this isn't the right moment for environmental outrage, she changes her tone. 'You could have come here,' she says, her voice tentative now, hopeful.

'I didn't want to wake you up.'

'I thought you'd been avoiding me.'

'Of course not.' They look each other in the eye, both of them aware it's a lie. 'Well, okay, yes, I have.'

'Was it the lesbian thing?'

'Shit, Helen, it would take more than a strap-on dildo to scare me off!' She sighs, the atmosphere in the room beginning to relax. 'It's what you said about Bob; about settling for what I've got. I don't have anything, that's the point. It doesn't matter if I never find happiness on my own.

I mean, I'm not happy now, so what do I have to lose?'

'I was just trying to be helpful.'

'God, I know that. And you're probably right. I mean, I've spent the last twenty years making bad decisions.'

'No, it's not that . . .' For a moment, it looks as though she wants to say more, but decides against it. Instead she offers Carol a plate of what appears to be rabbit food that's been kept damp for several months and then dried out in a temperamental oven.

'Home-made cookies. They're very healthy.'

'Yeah, they look it. Maybe later, thanks.'

Helen picks one up and takes a bite, razor-like shards of oat flakes tumbling down her sweater. What little she manages to get into her mouth takes twenty or thirty seconds to chew.

'They're probably better for dipping,' she says, at last free to speak again. 'So what time did you get home?'

'Oh, I don't know. Seven-thirty, eight. The sun was coming up. That's the only reason I stopped. It felt quite good to drive in circles in the dark, but somehow daylight just made it all seem sad.'

'Light shows us the truth of what we are.' She notices Carol's angry expression. 'I mean, the truth of our circumstances.' She tries dipping another cookie in her tea, but it instantly breaks away and sinks to the bottom of her cup as oaten sludge.

'At least I was back in the house when Bob woke up,' says Carol. 'I mean, imagine trying to explain the night to him.'

'Which part?'

'Oh, God, all of it.' She stares at the floor, too distracted to notice Helen dredging the gunk from her teacup and eating it in sloppy spoonfuls. 'The worst thing is the dream didn't just feel real, it felt right. Right that she was dead.'

'Well, you don't like her, do you?'

'And?'

'What?'

'I was hoping for more than a statement of the obvious. I thought you liked trying to interpret dreams.'

'I've read a couple of books about it, but that doesn't make me an expert.' Helen looks eager to change the subject. 'I just need to add some water,' she says, as she picks up the teapot and rushes from the room.

'How's Jane?'

'Staying with her father for a few weeks,' replies Helen, from the kitchen. 'That should be long enough to dispel the notion that he's perfect.'

'And long enough to make his new wife wonder what she's got herself into.'

'Well, I wasn't going to say it, but it has crossed my mind.' She reappears in the doorway, the faint sound of a kettle heating up in the background. 'What about Sophie? She must be getting suspicious by now.'

'We've told her we're both using up spare holiday before the end of the year. Her only question was why we couldn't use it in Italy. She looked very unimpressed when I offered to make spaghetti and said we could all just pretend.'

Helen laughs and returns to the kitchen. Alone again, Carol's thoughts drift back to the things that are troubling her.

'I think maybe the good thing about my dream last night is that I realize now I need to let go of the fantasies.'

'What do you mean?' calls Helen, out of sight.

'I think part of me has always believed things would work themselves out with my mother. That if I just kept at it, she'd miraculously transform into someone else, like her personality was just a bad case of the flu or something. I can see now it's never going to be better than this.'

She starts talking to the carpet as Helen returns. It feels easier to bare her soul to a mud-coloured shag pile, in the same way she can pour her thoughts on to a blank sheet of paper.

'It's like Bob, isn't it? I mean, part of our problem is this crazy belief I can only tell him what he wants to hear, but there's more to it than that. I've been waiting all these years for him to become something different, always telling myself, "Oh, I can't leave him just yet, he's about to go into his chrysalis stage. Everything will be okay after that." And the funny thing is he's not even a caterpillar, he's a slug.'

'How's he doing?'

'You can see for yourself. He's picking me up at eleven-thirty. There's a film he wants us to see – guns and explosions and lots of killing, as if his own cancer isn't enough.'

'Maybe it's a sort of allegorical thing. You know, for the fight ahead of him.'

'No, this is Bob we're talking about. He just likes crap, violent films.'

Outside, a wheelie-bin topples over in the wind, the sound echoing through the empty streets.

'Do you think he'll be okay in this weather?'

'God, yes. That's something else I've realized. Bob is like my mother: he's indestructible. I shouldn't even be worrying about the cancer. The man is probably immortal.'

Bob doesn't get out of the car when he arrives at Helen's, instead he just blows the car horn a couple of times.

'I sometimes think he's avoiding me,' says Helen, as they watch him through the living-room window.

'I wish he'd start avoiding me too.'

'Is he? Avoiding me, I mean.'

'Of course not, he's much too simple for that.' Helen looks unconvinced. 'I think he just assumes we do girly things together. It's a threat to his manliness to get too close.' She pulls her scarf tight and starts buttoning up her coat. 'And, of course, now he's only got one ball, his manhood has become a bit of an issue.'

'Well, give him my love, won't you?'

'In lieu of my own, gladly.' She gives Helen a hug. 'When you've had a chance to figure out what my dream meant, call me!'

'Nice morning?' says Bob.

'Not bad. She sends her greetings.'

'But she's a bit weird these days, isn't she?'

They both wave at Helen as the car pulls away.

'Her heart's in the right place,' says Carol. 'And she thinks very highly of you.'

'Really?' He looks surprised, as though he's now willing

to see Helen in a totally new light. 'But she doesn't know anything, right? About me, I mean.'

'No, no, of course not. We're always too busy talking about her problems to talk about yours.'

Bob nears the end of Helen's street, approaching the junction with an unusual attention to detail. He applies the brake calmly, slowly, positioning the car at a precise right angle to the dotted white lines.

Carol has noticed this change in recent days, a need for order in even the simplest tasks. A perfectly boiled egg is no longer just an egg, it's a symbol of triumph over the odds, in the same way that a badly ironed shirt is now a harbinger of doom and chaos.

They pull on to a busier road, Bob continuing to drive at an almost ceremonial pace, carefully centred in the middle of the lane.

He glances down at the dashboard and instantly looks confused. 'The tank's almost empty. I could swear I filled it up a couple of days ago.'

'It doesn't matter, we'll get some more on the way.'

He's still frowning at the petrol gauge, the edges of his world clearly becoming blurred and disorderly.

'Forget about it. You've had a lot on your mind.' She rubs his leg affectionately, the same way she might comfort an incontinent dog that's just pissed indoors. Before she even knows what she's saying, meaningless words of affection bubble up to her lips. 'Don't worry about it, Bob. I still love you.'

53

TECHNICALLY SPEAKING, ALBERT isn't giving up, he's merely postponing the search. But postponing until when? He's chilled to the bone and winter has barely begun.

When he eventually finds a bus home, he happily takes a seat downstairs; his heels are so badly blistered, he would sooner walk home than climb to the upper deck.

So this is what it's come to, he thinks, as he rides beside an old man who smells of peppermints and urine. I'm looking old, feeling old, and now I'm acting old too.

Like his fellow passengers, he gazes out of the window absent-mindedly, no longer certain whether the bus is moving or if it's the world outside that is passing them by.

He's so distracted by his aches and pains and fears, he doesn't notice the flag at first. It's some way off, barely cresting the rooftops, and yet the wind is snapping at it with such violence, it demands attention.

Even when he actually sees it, he still doesn't connect the dots. It's just a flag – and in this wind! Watching it struggle against its tether, Albert can imagine it might come ripping free at any moment, soaring above the rooftops and floating away to who knows where?

'Bloody hell!' No longer aware of his pain, he leaps up and rings the bell. 'I've got to get off!' he shouts.

'At the next stop,' the driver replies angrily.

They've barely left the last one, and Albert is in no mood to add another mile to his journey.

'I'm going to piss myself,' he replies, loud enough for everyone to hear. 'I think it might be the squirts as well.'

The driver hurriedly pulls over, the other passengers quietly murmuring their thanks that they aren't yet at Albert's stage.

As the bus pulls away, he's confident which direction the flag is in, but when he gets deeper into the estate, its labyrinth of avenues and cul-de-sacs quickly begins to baffle him. He turns a corner only to find a dead end, and then tries to retrace his steps only to find another dead end. The weather means there's no one on the streets to ask for directions, and even when he comes across a young boy on a bicycle, the conversation doesn't go as planned.

'I'm looking for a flagpole,' says Albert.

'You what?'

'A flagpole.' He tries to indicate something tall and erect, though in retrospect he realizes his choice of hand gestures may have been ill considered.

'You total perv.'

'I think I should be going.'

The boy watches him walk away. 'I'll show you mine if you show me yours.'

Albert ignores him, quickening his pace now, turning left and right at random. Just as he thinks he'll never even find his way out, let alone find Connie, wham! He turns another corner and there it is, a world straight from her letters, more like a film set than a place where real people live. It isn't quite as he'd imagined it, but there's no doubting this is the place. And towering over it all, the flagpole makes it feel like its own little kingdom, independent of the outside world.

Up this close, he's more convinced than ever that the flag will be torn free at any second. It snaps back and forth in the wind, its seams beginning to fray.

He turns to face the opposite house – Connie's. That's surely the ultimate proof that he belongs here. That he knows exactly which house is hers; its front garden plain but tidy; its double-glazed windows keeping them all snug against the elements.

He straightens his coat and does his best to walk towards the front door with a purposeful, authoritative gait. Although he's not on official Royal Mail business, his heart is beating so fast, he needs something to steel himself with. He imagines he's actually calling to explain the latest parcel rates, or to introduce a new scheme in which retiring postmen are made available as friends to unhappy housewives.

As he listens to the ring of the doorbell, it feels as if the sound is for him as much as Connie. It signals the start of something; not the end of a journey but the beginning of a new one.

From behind him, the sound of footsteps. Albert turns to see Mandy hurrying across the cul-de-sac in high heels.

'Bob and Carol are out. Can I sign for it?' She gets close enough to see his empty hands and instantly looks crestfallen. Even Albert glances down at himself, ashamed now that he hadn't borrowed a Royal Mail bag to complete the look.

'Hello, I . . .' He struggles to find something to say. Seeing her standing here, someone who knows Connie, he's gripped by a need to bare his soul, to tell her everything.

'I'm here for Connie—'

Mandy looks blank. 'Carol.'

They stare at one another.

'You mean Carol,' she says again.

Her real name! In the heavens above, angels don't just sing, they carouse and order another round for everyone.

'Carol,' he says. 'Yes, that's right. Carol has some . . . some undelivered mail. We, er, we no longer return it for . . . for budgetary reasons. So I wanted to tell her she should . . . she should come and collect it.'

Mandy appears unconcerned that a postman is calling on a Sunday and using Carol's first name. 'Not to worry,' she says. 'I'll tell her.'

'Oh, you don't need to do that. I'm often in the area. I'll drop by another time.'

Mandy looks relieved, as if she knows she wouldn't have remembered. She starts to totter back across the street.

'Excuse me,' shouts Albert. 'How do I get out to the main road?'

Again, Mandy seems to take the question in her stride,

clearly finding nothing unusual in a postman who's lost. 'You have to keep going left,' she says uncertainly. 'I mean, right. Well, both, actually, but not in that order.' She blushes. 'Hold on, it helps if I think of doing it in the car.'

She takes hold of an imaginary steering-wheel and begins driving, even taking care occasionally to change gear. She seems far away now, barely even aware that she's standing in the middle of the street. Watching her, Albert feels as though he's consulting some kind of spirit medium: she's entered a trance and at any moment will start spewing ectoplasm.

'Okay,' she says, her gaze fixed on the middle distance, 'it's left . . .' More imaginary driving. 'Then left again . . .' She frowns, perhaps stuck behind a slow driver or dodging an imaginary child. 'Then it's right. And then you're there.'

'Left, left, right. Thanks very much.'

'Like a dance, isn't it? Left, left, right.' She turns back towards her house, her shock of blonde hair reminding Albert of a rabbit running for cover.

'Toodle-pip,' she shouts, as she wobbles up her driveway and out of sight.

54

MONDAY MORNING, THE day of Bob's test results, and the weekend's gales have died away, bright sunshine at least giving the appearance of warmth. Now that Bob is a closet follower of omens, Carol is just relieved she can drive him to the specialist without the weather making it appear as if the world is coming to an end.

They don't talk in the car, don't even have the radio on. They tried at the very start of the journey – turning left, left and right while Carol focused on driving in a duly auspicious manner – but every joke and every song sounded puerile against the backdrop of their day. Silence is the only thing that feels appropriate.

The roads thicken with rush-hour traffic as they edge closer to central London, the world around them bumper to bumper in shirt sleeves and dark suits. Moments like this always remind Carol of a time they went on holiday at rush-hour, heading for Heathrow as the rest of the world crawled to work. She'd felt special back then, as though she had a secret she wanted to share – a delicious urge to wind down the window and tell people she'd be on the beach by the end of the day, that she'd spend the next two weeks drinking cocktails and thinking of their daily grind.

Now here they are again, inching through traffic with a different kind of secret. It makes her wonder how many things she'll never know about the people around her: how the businessman in the car to her left perhaps isn't going to the office at all, but is instead just going through the motions, still unable to accept that he was laid off last month; and how the woman in the car behind maybe isn't taking her young children to school, but rather to say goodbye to their father, dying with kidney disease.

'Doesn't this seem perverse to you?'

It's obvious Bob isn't expecting conversation. 'What's perverse?' he says, his face creased from pondering his own thoughts.

'The way we all live. I mean, we travel through life hemmed in like this, brushing up against each other, and yet we know nothing about each other's lives.'

'And what exactly do you want to know about other people's lives?'

'Where they're going. What they're doing. How they feel about it.'

Bob does a quick tally of the cars around them. 'Work, work, work, school maybe, and I don't know, but it can't be anything fun because she looks miserable.'

'Wouldn't you like to know why she looks sad? Maybe you can help her feel better.'

'Are you feeling all right?'

'Yes, I'm—'

'I'm happy to drive, you know.'

'No, I'm just . . . I mean, wouldn't you like these people to know you're going to hospital?'

'No.'

'But imagine if they all knew, all these people wishing you well.'

'Feeling sorry for me, you mean. Everyone thinking, Poor sod, he'll be dead before Christmas.'

His words hang heavily in the still air of the car. Clearly unnerved, he turns the radio back on. The breakfast DJ and his team now sound so hyper, it's easy to believe they've been snorting something between tracks. It's inane and stupefying, and undeniable that Bob is hating every second of it.

'Look,' says Carol, 'I'm sorry I mentioned it.'

'No, no, it's fine.'

'At least turn the radio off.'

'But I'm enjoying it.'

'Of course you're not. I won't say anything else, I promise.'

'No, it's nice to have some music.' She sees him wince as Britney Spears comes on, clogging the airwaves with aural fluff. 'It's just something to pass the time, isn't it?'

'Look, we both hate Britney.' She switches to a different station. The car fills with the sombre tones of Chopin's funeral march. 'Okay, well, maybe not this . . .' She changes station again just in time to hear a country singer wailing about his best friend dying.

Bob quickly turns it back to Britney, who by now is

crooning about teenage angst in a song that could easily be called 'Slap Me, I Need It'.

At the far end of the gridlocked street, traffic lights shine green, their function reduced to a mere taunt.

While Britney continues her musical assault, Carol and Bob simply wait it out, the omens looking less and less auspicious by the second.

After a protracted journey that felt more like root-canal treatment, Carol is at least looking forward to seeing the receptionist again, but it's a different woman today: older and more matronly, with the puffy appearance of someone who drinks on the sly – a look that Carol knows well.

As usual, however, Bob's specialist is in fine form, giving them such a broad smile as they enter, Carol can register nothing but his perfect white teeth.

'Good morning!' He shakes Bob's hand with genuine warmth. 'And, Mrs Cooper, it's wonderful to meet you again.'

As they all sit down, however, he literally turns the smile off. 'I have to tell you,' he says, 'I'm afraid it's not good news.'

55

IF GLORIA COULD understand Albert's words, she'd be tired of hearing about his expedition by now – the size of Carol's house, for instance, 'nothing ostentatious, just lovely,' and her crazy neighbour, 'mad as a fruitcake, and "toodle-pip" of all things, but she was lovely too'. Every statement is a rheumy-eyed reminiscence, as though he's recounting an entire summer spent with dear friends.

He wants to go back and see Carol today, but it's a Monday – the start of his final week at work – and he feels an obligation to be there. This is a new feeling for him, to think of the job as an obligation rather than a privilege. The postal service had meant something to him once, but that was back when he'd also meant something to it. Now the job is just an inconvenience; a distraction from his budding social life.

Still, a few more days won't hurt. For a start, he knows where to find Carol now, so there's really no hurry. On a more practical level, his feet look like something from a butcher's block and he's worried he might have to take his shoes off in

Carol's house. Blood-stained socks don't seem like the best start to a rich and rewarding friendship.

He doesn't notice the aching at first. He feels a little tired, but he dismisses that as too much exercise over the weekend. It's only as the day wears on that he realizes something is wrong. His thoughts have been full of Carol, but now she's receding into a fog. He tries to hold on to her – and the house and the flagpole and the crazy woman across the street – but it's all slipping away, fading out of sight.

He pulls on his coat, suddenly aware that he's chilled to the bone, his whole body leaden and stiff.

'Going somewhere?' says Mickey.

'Home.'

'Ah, you lucky bastard.'

Despite the filthy state of the lift, Albert leans against the wall to steady himself. The journey home has been surreal, the world around him seemingly reduced to slow motion, so that every step, every movement, has felt disconnected and eternal. Now here he is, arriving home at last, but to a flat without food for him or Gloria.

The lift doors open and Max's flowers come into view, a gaudy burst of colour that's more like a migraine than a garden.

There's still no sign of Max. Now that he doesn't need to water his plants, he seems to spend all his time indoors, the curtains drawn shut.

Albert glances in Max's window as he passes, but only

sees his own reflection: an old man, his face pale and drawn.

Gloria looks relieved when he walks through the door. Her nest of toilet tissue is stained yellow with piss, but Albert can't make it that far.

'I'm sorry,' he says, as he crumples on to the sofa. 'I just need to lie down for a while . . .'

They watch one another, two old friends on opposite sides of the room, each of them immobile and stricken.

'I'll see to you in just a little while,' he says, his eyes already beginning to close. 'In just a little while, I promise . . .'

56

THE NEWS OF Bob's diagnosis blasts through Carol's life with such force she's certain that a part of her will be for ever imprinted on the walls of the specialist's office.

The rest of their time there is dedicated to treatment plans and prognoses, everything presented in the same optimistic tone as before, but it rings hollow now. She and Bob are tumbling to earth, spinning, disoriented, and no one can tell them how far they will have to fall or even whether their parachute will open.

There are firm handshakes and words of reassurance as they leave his office, but this time his smile is tinged with sympathy and there's no talk of gin.

Outside, it seems fitting to find London bathed in the watery sunlight of an English winter's day, as though the sky is saturated with the tears she and Bob feel but don't yet know how to shed.

They try going for lunch, not because they're hungry but because it feels familiar, something to prove that their world isn't really coming to an end. A crowded café off the King's Road isn't perhaps the best choice, hemmed in by the kind of people whose definition of stress is having no downtime between lunch and a pedicure.

Bob and Carol sit in silence, not eating the food in front of them, not even touching their drinks.

'It's going to be okay,' says Carol, softly.

Bob doesn't reply, just reaches for her hand, almost no room for it between the plates of uneaten chicken salad and pots of lemon-grass tea.

They stay like this, squeezing each other's hands tighter and tighter, desperately wanting to chase the evil away.

Bob's tears are barely noticeable at first, but as his shoulders begin to shake and he slowly hunches forward, nearby diners start to speak more quietly. Table by table, it ripples across the room, until Bob's sobbing is the only sound, the whole café gripped by the awkward silence of people who no longer know what to say or do.

57

WHEN ALBERT WAKES up, he can't remember where he is. The room looks different in the half-light of dawn, and he feels so weary, so unlike his usual self.

'I'm dreaming,' he whispers, his mouth dry and gritty.

He waits for the dream to play itself out: for the ceiling to become a bed of daffodils, perhaps, or for his wife to come and dance for him on the back of an elephant.

But it doesn't happen.

Nothing happens.

It's only as the cool light of morning creeps deeper into the room and Gloria starts to cry that he realizes this is real. He tries to get up, but can barely lift his head from the sofa.

'I'm in a bit of a state,' he says feebly.

Gloria calls back to him from her piss-stained nest, clearly confused as to why he isn't cleaning her, feeding her, loving her.

'Look at us both. What a pair we make.'

He can see the telephone on the coffee-table, probably within reach if he tries hard enough.

I could wait, he thinks. Maybe the worst is over. Maybe in an hour or two I'll be tottering about and making a cup of tea.

But then he glances back at Gloria and he knows things won't get better. There's a panicked look in her eyes, an instinctive recognition of the danger they're in. No one will miss him for days, he knows that. They'll both be dead by then.

If he can reach the phone . . . and yet he's scared. There's only one number he can call and it's the ultimate surrender; a call that will bring strangers barging into his home. He knows how the system works, how it chews up helpless old men and their sick cats.

What he wants is to call Carol. She'd come straight round, he's sure of that. She'd take care of Gloria's bed and do whatever else needed to be done. That's the kind of girl she is.

'I'm frightened,' he gasps, his eyes welling up now.

Wincing through his tears, he strains for the phone, every bone in his body aching from the effort.

Slowly he leans out from the sofa, edges closer and closer. With inches to go, he slips and falls against the table, gashing his face open and knocking the phone to the floor.

Albert doesn't hear the front door being kicked in; he is only aware of other people as the paramedics prise the phone from his hand and lift him onto a stretcher.

'And Gloria,' he mumbles. 'My cat . . .'

'Don't worry, your neighbours will look after the cat.'

'No, they'll kill her! They'll kill her!' He can feel the stretcher moving beneath him, a sensation of flying. He sees Gloria watching them leave. 'You don't understand, she's sick too . . .'

Gloria becomes a wall, and a broken door, then a rush of cold air. Albert wants to sit up, wants to demand they go back. Instead, he finds himself floating past Max's flowers at head height, suddenly aware that their plastic petals are already beginning to gather dust.

58

IT'S BEEN A long night. While Bob has slept soundly beside her, Carol has stared at the ceiling, the hours passing in a slow accumulation of seconds. As she listens to the steady rise and fall of Bob's breathing – the man she's spent nearly twenty years with, the father of her child – she finds herself doing something she's never expected: trying to strike a bargain with the universe, offering whatever she can so that he may live a long and happy life.

Sacrificing her own happiness sounds like a very grand gesture, but she's been doing that for years; taking depreciation into account, it's probably a pretty worthless offer by now. So what's left? There's only her own life, the one bargaining chip that still has any currency.

It's an odd thought, that she'd be willing to die if only he could live, but it's true. Not because she loves him – though her pity feels so love-like right now, she can almost kid herself that she has fallen back in love with him – but simply because, lying here in the dead of night, his life seems to have more value than hers. He isn't confused and conflicted; he doesn't regret the choices he's made. If single-celled organisms can be said to live with integrity, then Bob is a good and righteous man. In his simplicity, in his patent transparency, he is everything that Carol is not. Even as a parent he's more valuable than her. If Sophie has to be left with just one of them, it would be better him than her, they all know that.

Carol still doesn't know how they're going to break the news to Sophie. She and Bob have agreed that the time has come, if only because they won't be able to keep it a secret for much longer, but how? They want to be reassuring when they tell her, but neither of them feels capable of that just yet. Telling Sophie will have to wait until they can at least look and sound as if they believe what they're saying.

Helen so rarely visits Carol's house that the sight of her walking up the driveway only confirms what Carol feels in her heart: the world is rapidly disintegrating into something unpredictable and unknowable.

Even Helen appears bewildered to be here, the way Carol remembers people looking at the airport, everyone dazed and jetlagged but determined to put a brave face on it.

'Do you mind me turning up like this?' she says, as Carol leads her into the living room.

'Christ, of course not! You're always welcome.'

'It's just I couldn't get hold of you yesterday. Or this morning. I thought you'd stopped talking to me again.'

'It's Bob . . .' She lowers her voice, unsure where he is. 'We got the results back yesterday.' Before she can even think of how to phrase the next line, Helen is there, enfolding her in an embrace that feels so warm, so right, Carol doesn't know how she's survived for twenty-four hours without it.

'Has it spread far?'

'Far enough.'

'He can beat this, you know that.'

'We're still working on saying it right now. Believing it will come next.' She smiles sadly. 'Look, sit down, I'll make a drink.'

'You don't need to.'

'No, I want to.' And it's true, that's all she wants right now: demands placed upon her, the needs of others to erase all awareness of her own. As she fusses over a cafetière, she catches sight of her reflection in the kitchen window, ghostlike against the grey backdrop of a damp suburban cul-de-sac. It isn't even a face she recognizes any more: it's that of a junkie desperate for oblivion.

She turns off the light, exorcizes the vision. 'I'm sorry it's not herbal,' she says, as she carries a tray through to the living room.

'Caffeine's bad for you, do you know that?'

'So are these.' She offers her a plate of chocolate biscuits. 'I didn't make them. Which is why they're edible.'

'Well, maybe just one . . .'

'See how the mighty fall.'

Bob enters the room, his approach so silent Carol assumes he's been eavesdropping.

'Right, Helen?' He looks uncomfortable at the sight of

someone else in the house. 'Carol didn't tell me you were coming over.'

'She didn't know. It was a surprise visit.' Bob frowns, his eyes darting from Helen to Carol and back to Helen again. 'I thought Carol had been avoiding me,' she adds. 'Turned out I was just going mad.'

He nods now, as though he's been aware of this for some time. 'I'm popping down the DIY store,' he says to Carol. 'The shelves in the bathroom are a bit loose. I thought I could fix them and paint the wall while I'm at it.'

Helen beams at him a little too broadly. 'You can start on my house next.'

Without a smile, without a word, he leaves the room.

'Welcome to our strange new reality,' says Carol, as the front door closes behind him.

'How are you holding up?'

'Oh, don't. I feel guilty even asking myself that question. I mean, it's not me who's sick, is it?'

'But your feelings still matter.'

'Do they?' She says it with an anger that takes both of them by surprise. Helen looks away, and for a brief instant Carol is certain she can see a guilty expression on her face.

59

ALBERT HAS BEEN inspected and injected and even now there's a drip stuck in his hand. Yet as the threat of death appears to recede, in its place comes the much greater fear that his carefully organized life has just been blown to Hell.

Gloria is already dead, he's certain of that, and it doesn't take much imagination to think what would happen to a council flat in South London with no front door. The place probably looks like Haiti by now: plundered and looted beyond description, everything he's ever held dear either stolen or simply tossed into the street. His wife's clothes. Her pillow.

He can feel his eyes welling up again.

'Stop it,' he says sternly. If men aren't supposed to cry, there's certainly no excuse for it after all these years of practice. It's simply that everything about his life appears so fragile now – how he's struggled to preserve a filigree of happiness, unaware that it was always a lost cause. This is a cruel and unkind world, too hard and savage for gossamer lives like his.

There's some comfort in remembering that most people on his estate aren't inclined to read, possibly don't even know how, so Carol's letters are probably safer than everything else in the flat, but their sanctity would still have been defiled. The biscuit tin was his to open and his alone.

'Bastards,' he says to himself.

'What's that, love?' A nurse pushes back the curtain surrounding his bed. 'Gracious, why all the tears? We're here to help you.'

'I know,' he says, already feeling ashamed. 'It's . . . it's nothing.'

She fusses over his pillows, her scent a blend of soap and fabric softener. 'Your social worker will be here in a little while.'

Albert stiffens. Social workers are for people who've fallen through the cracks, people who are damned never to get out again. Even the idea of having a social worker suggests chronic helplessness; the ultimate statement that his life is no longer his own.

'I don't think that will be necessary,' he says.

'Well,' she replies, with a laugh, 'you can tell them that when they come, can't you?'

Pat isn't a woman so much as a force of nature. In the moments before she arrives, Albert can almost feel her approach, like a Tube train pushing a wall of air before it.

'Albert!' she exclaims, as she throws the curtains back. 'I'm Pat. It's wonderful to meet you.'

She speaks in a thick Welsh accent, so that every syllable

269

sounds jubilant, as though she might break into song at any moment.

'Do I know you?' he replies.

'You do now! I'm your social worker.' She sits down beside him and takes hold of his hand. 'You're probably going to be in here for a few more days. How are you feeling?'

'Is Gloria dead?' He chokes up, desperate not to start crying again.

Pat looks blank.

'Gloria's my cat.'

'Dead? Of course she's not dead! I mean, the poor thing looks like something from the British Museum, but she's definitely not dead.'

It takes Albert a few moments to process what she's saying. More than anything, it's her smile that reassures him. This woman is a walking ray of sunshine. 'So where is she?'

'Well, it took some doing, but we managed to find her a foster home, so everything's okay now.' She says it with an air of hesitancy, as if the intervening steps were fraught with chaos – that Gloria was shunted from place to place, perhaps briefly went missing altogether.

'And you're sure we're talking about the same cat?'

'Ageing tabby? Two broken legs? I know London has it all, but I suspect you've cornered the market with that one.'

'I take good care of her.'

'Well, anyone can see that.'

'She was only sitting in her own filth because I couldn't get to her.'

'Of course she was. She's a lovely cat – a credit to you.'

She fishes in her bag, pulls out a bunch of keys. 'Your door's already been fixed.'

'Was anything stolen?'

'That kind of thing doesn't happen on my watch, Albert!' She gives him another smile. 'If it's okay with you, I'll keep hold of them until you're ready . . . Goodness, why are you crying?'

'I thought they'd put me in a home or something. You know, give my flat to Romanians.'

'Over my big fat dead body. Don't let the smile fool you, Albert. I can eat a whole sheep in one bite, woolly coat and all.'

Albert smiles through his tears.

'My,' she says, 'what beautiful teeth!'

'And they're all real,' he replies, with a blush.

'See, Albert, you're just like me. You're a miracle worker. Between the two of us, we'll take over the world!'

60

Bob's hospital doesn't look or feel like a hotel any more. It doesn't help that Carol is no longer a mere visitor, and Bob is no longer there as the-man-with-one-less-bollock, problem-solved.

She hadn't remembered the bright lights and the sterility, the near-silent pacing of nurses in sensible shoes. As they're led to a private room, Carol notices a middle-aged woman quietly weeping, her grief no less poignant for its discretion. Just as quickly she's gone, blocked from view by the gentle closing of a door.

After a long silence in which Carol and Bob are able to take in every detail of his room – the easy-wipe surfaces, everything suggestive of a place where self-mastery comes to die – a nurse enters and Bob's time has come: the needle, the puncturing of a vein, and finally the intravenous drip, the steady percolation of chemicals that signal the real war has now begun.

While they wait, Bob flicks through past issues of *GQ*,

discreetly lingering over the inevitable female models. Carol had expected him to be more emotional than this, had expected him to need her, as a child needs a parent – isn't that why she's come, why they've stayed together all these years? In the absence of his hysteria, her own seems to magnify. She wants to smash something, to hyperventilate, to run screaming through the corridors until someone medicates her and makes the pain go away.

All these years she's wished Bob ill, and now she wants to save him but is helpless, both of them plummeting earthward on a journey she shouldn't even be on.

Just when she thinks she can't take it any longer, that either she or the hospital will be consumed by flames, it's all over – a smiling nurse is escorting them to the main entrance and waving goodbye as if they're old friends who really just popped in for a cup of tea and a chat.

From the moment they get home, Carol stays in the kitchen, staring at the floor as her mind crumbles, but always managing to appear busy when Bob comes into the room.

Afraid that he may lose his appetite as the chemotherapy progresses, Bob has begun acting like an animal preparing for winter, stocking up on calories whenever and wherever he can find them. On this, his third visit to the kitchen, he slowly pads around the room pilfering what little food remains. Here a slice of ham, there a stale doughnut.

He lingers by the window. 'It's all beginning to unravel, isn't it?'

'What did you say?'

He points across the street, where the neighbour's flag is beginning to fray in a fresh surge of wind. Carol watches it flap back and forth, its edges slowly disintegrating into shreds of red, white and blue.

'I need to go out,' she says.

'Do you want some company?'

'No, I just need to go shopping.' She knows that's a safe thing to say. Suggesting Bob come shopping is like asking a vampire to eat garlic. Now that every moment in his life has presumably taken on new meaning, she can easily imagine he'll never want to set foot in a shop again.

'Well, I might leave you to that,' he says, as he opens a can of Coke and wanders from the room. 'Spend a little time on my computer instead.'

She listens to his footsteps, her heart beating faster now.

She's just lied. To a man with cancer. Technically she's been doing this for some time, but today it's a conscious and wilful act, done in full knowledge of his condition. It's the beginning of a treachery she's certain she'll regret but feels powerless to stop.

The travel agent is friendly, but noticeably less so than on previous occasions. She eyes Carol suspiciously as she hammers at her computer, each key stroke a sharp, angry jab.

'Do you think you'll actually go this time?' She glances at the customers at the next desk, evidently in the mood to play to an audience. 'I mean, I can take your money, but it seems a waste if you're just going to cancel again. You book, you cancel, you book, you cancel—'

'My husband has cancer.'

This doesn't explain why she's going away on her own, but the truth of her words is written across her face; even she knows that.

Everyone nods awkwardly and tries their best not to look at one another. Even Carol's agent begins typing quietly, her long, brightly coloured fingernails ill suited to subtlety.

And all the while the same thought keeps going over and over in Carol's head. *I am a bad woman.* She's waited all these years for the right moment to leave Bob only to pick the very worst instead. Yet doing the right thing doesn't even seem to be an option any more – there is no right thing; just degrees of pain, of selfishness, of hurt.

On the way home she tries to atone with a trip to the supermarket and dedicates the entire experience to Bob. It's a feeble gesture, she understands that, but there's some comfort in knowing that the cupboards will be brimming with all his favourite food long after she's gone.

By the time Carol gets home, Bob is so engaged in World of Warcraft, he seems incapable of real-life interaction. Even when he takes a brief break to re-feed, he appears unconcerned that Carol has come home with fifteen bags of food exclusively for him.

'Wow, it's my lucky day,' he says, as he opens a packet of iced buns. He holds one between his teeth, keeping his hands free for two cans of Coke and a packet of processed cheese, then wanders back to the living room.

This rhythmic ebb and flow of junk food and online sloth

characterizes the rest of the evening, so that by ten-thirty he's a physical wreck, not even fit for staring at a computer screen.

'I think you should go to bed,' says Carol.

'Maybe you're right. What time are you turning in?'

'Later. I just want to clear my head.'

Even after he shuffles from the room, Carol sits motionless, waits until she's certain he's in bed. Then, moving with the kind of stealth that can only exist in the presence of guilt, she turns on her computer . . .

Richard's picture doesn't do him justice, she can see that now. The truth of him, the life of him – a camera can't capture those things. All that remains of the man she remembers is his smile, hurriedly snapped in the back of a cab when their life together seemed thrilling and unshakeable.

She zooms in on the picture, closing in on a face she's known and loved and kissed, and held and longed for. She zooms in closer and closer until his right eye fills the whole screen; a pixelated, distorted image of something she's lost.

Still unsure how to say what needs to be said – what has been left unsaid for too many years – she picks up a pen and begins to write.

61

IT'S NICE TO be back, and it doesn't matter that the day is cold and grey. That's the thing about a graveyard. It doesn't depend on sunlight and beauty to do its job. If anything, there's a shared sympathy in sitting beside Richard's grave like this, the cold creeping through the soles of Carol's shoes, slowly numbing her feet.

She can still remember the day she got the news, the way it drifted to her weeks after the event. That the man she loved had died. That she hadn't even known he was sick. That she would never get a chance to say goodbye.

It's been a long time since she's come here. She used to come a lot in the early days, but it didn't help. Didn't help her and certainly didn't help him. There are only a certain number of times you can apologize to a gravestone before you realize it's too late.

It was Helen who saved her. After watching her dissolve with grief, still in her twenties, a young child to care for, it was Helen who eventually convinced her that she had to let go.

But she hadn't really let go, had she? Part of her had stayed here in this graveyard all these years, quietly remembering the past, longing to have it back again, to have a chance to do it all differently.

She can't help thinking it would have been better if she really had stayed here. Maybe it would have made her a better person, a better mother. At least she would have stood for something; at least she would have been true to herself.

'Where's Carol?' people would say.

'Down in the graveyard, of course', as if it's the most natural thing in the world for a young woman to dedicate the rest of her life to a granite headstone.

She could have ended her days a gnarled old lady, still camped beside Richard's grave, weather-beaten and eccentric, as much a fixture as the dead themselves, but an oddly comforting presence to mourners visiting nearby graves.

'Sorry,' says Carol, as she wipes the dirt from Richard's gravestone, 'I've been neglecting you.'

She blushes, still bashful in his presence.

'But you're looking well, all things considered.'

She instinctively gives him time to respond, smiling at the silence because it's his.

'I've written to Sophie. It's probably the ramblings of a madwoman, but I think it's a step forward. It makes me sound a bit of a whore, to be honest – that I was a married mother when I fell in love with you – but she needs to know what I've given up for her. Otherwise nothing about the last fifteen years makes any sense. Maybe there's even something she can learn in there, that if you live your entire life trying to keep everybody else happy, you just end up disappointing everyone, including yourself.

'I know I should sit her down and do it all face to face, but . . .' She sighs, the chaos of her life threatening to spoil the visit. 'So I'm just going to post it to her. She has her own post-office box, no less. It's supposed to be a teenage thing, something to do with privacy, though I don't know why she bothers. I'm sure the only mail she gets is from Mensa—' She stops herself. 'See? This is the kind of mother I am – sniping and resentful. All my dreams come true.'

She glances around, no one in sight.

'I need a hug, do you mind?'

Trying not to get her coat dirty, she sits down and leans back against the headstone, slowly at first, terrified it may topple, but it feels rooted and steady behind her, the same feeling she used to get lying against him in bed. Relaxing with the memory, she rests her head against the cold granite, imagines having Richard back, right here on the damp ground. To have him wrapped around her. In her.

'I realized something last night. When I decided to stay with Bob, I was basically saying it's okay to raise a child in a loveless home. On that basis, I'd failed as a mother when I'd barely begun. It's taken me all these years to figure that out.'

A flock of birds passes overhead, stark against the grey sky. Watching them fly into the distance, she finds her thoughts reeling skyward with them, drifting freely now between past and present, life and death.

'Sophie saw your picture the other day. It reminded me of that day in the park . . .' She smiles at the memory, at the elaborate lengths she'd gone to in order to cover her tracks; finding a park so far from Croydon and everyone she knew that they'd spent most of the day getting there and back. And yet the subterfuge had been part of the fun, and even the journey had been a pleasure because they were together, appearing in public as if they were the proud young parents of their own beautiful child.

'Sophie liked you, I remember that . . .' Even as she hears herself say it, she can taste its bitter edge, a truth she's spent years trying to deny. Sophie needed her real father: wasn't that the point of the last eighteen years? And yet, looking back, it's so obvious they could have taken that one day in the park and spun it into a thousand more just like it: Richard loving Sophie as if she were his own, and Sophie cooing contentedly because she knew she was with happy people.

And Carol *was* happy: she can admit that now. Happy with Richard, of course, but happy with Sophie too. Mother and daughter playing together without a care in the world.

'I want to marry you.' That's what he'd said that day, as the three of them lay there on the grass.

'I'm already married.'

'No, you're not. You're just existing. – I'm asking you to live. You and Sophie and me.' It was testament to his character that Richard could make an indictment of her entire life and yet say it with a smile. 'Divorce him. Marry me.'

'Can we honeymoon in Athens?'

'Ah, romance among the ancients . . .'

'I want to see the Parthenon. To kiss you at the Parthenon.'

280

Now, as then, Bob starts to tear into the moment, brings her crashing back to the cold ground of a damp graveyard, the man she loved reduced to a lump of stone behind her. She fiddles with her wedding ring, aware that time is slipping through her fingers, as always.

'Bob has cancer. Though thankfully it's not the same type you had. I sometimes wonder if the universe is trying to tell me something. Though it should really tell the men in my life instead: "Don't fall in love with this woman, you'll die."

'I think I've been trying to look after him to make up for what I couldn't do for you. What I wasn't around to do for you.' She smiles sadly. 'It's odd when you think about it. I've spent all these years regretting I wasn't widowed before my thirtieth birthday and yet part of me still thinks you wouldn't have died if I'd been there for you.'

She takes a deep breath, tries to push the memories back to a place where the pain is dulled and tolerable.

'That's why I wrote the letter to Sophie, to set the record straight. To let her know it was never her fault how everything turned out, it was mine. The truth is I stopped being able to love anyone the day I left you.'

62

OFFICIALLY IT'S ALBERT'S last day at work, but everyone knows he's already gone. Albert's absence is conspicuous only to Albert himself. For everyone else, it's just another day.

As usual, the sorting machine thunders away in the middle of the room, sifting through envelopes with a rapid-fire omniscience. Even if Albert had been there this morning, he wouldn't have seen Carol's letter fly through the machine: the envelope emblazoned in her distinctive hand, but this time with Sophie's name and address rather than a smiley face.

In an instant, the letter is sorted and guaranteed safe passage from dusty backroom Purgatory.

In that respect, Albert has always been right about the machine: it is the keeper of secrets.

63

No CHECK-IN BAGGAGE. It's not just appropriate, it's necessary, vital. What's the point of going away if she's just going to drag along a suitcase full of her old life? So she'll only take a small bag, enough to get by for a few days, until she figures out what to do next.

This, of course, will also allow her to slip away from the house unnoticed, though even as she counts down the minutes to her departure, she still kids herself that she's going to tell Bob. They will have a calm, rational conversation about her need to end the marriage, and then she will head for the airport with a clear conscience, knowing – in some small way – that she's done the right thing.

She slowly makes a cup of coffee, aware that this is the last time she'll be using this kettle, this spoon, this kitchen. Every moment feels loaded with meaning now, the passing seconds adding more and more weight to even the simplest acts. Another ten minutes and she can imagine the entire world will collapse under the strain of it all.

Bob is at the dining table as usual, engrossed in his other reality. Watching him, Carol finds herself surprised at the tenderness of her feelings. Here is a man who visually, mentally and emotionally has been little more than a disappointment for their entire married life, yet at this exact moment she wants only to protect him, to wrap him up in cotton wool and tuck him away somewhere safe and warm so he can live the rest of his days in peace.

She sits down opposite him, the table between them strewn with empty Coke cans and stale bread crusts – a portent of what his life is about to become.

Five more minutes.

I'm still going to tell him.

'I'm going out in a moment.'

'Yeah?' He glances up at her, glassy-eyed and monosyllabic.

'Will you be all right on your own?'

'Course.' He turns his attention back to the computer, saving princesses and vanquishing evil in a world where everything is far simpler and more clear-cut than it is in real life.

'Okay,' she says. 'Well . . . see you.'

She stands up, still lingers by the table, unsure now if she can really go through with this, but Bob is so preoccupied, he doesn't even notice.

64

THERE'S A RHYTHM to hospital life that reminds Albert of the army. They're not woken up with a bugle at five in the morning and he doesn't have to make his own bed, but still there's a fixed pattern to the day that allows him to gauge the time just by listening to what's going on: the doctors doing their rounds, the meals being served, the visitors drifting in and out.

Pat isn't free to see him today, so he's spent the morning trying to read a book from the ward library, *The Man in the Mask*, though the more he reads, the less appropriate it seems for people who are essentially prisoners themselves.

'Catching up on reading, Albert?'

Darren stands beside his bed, looking a little lost without his clipboard and departmental authority. There's also something stiff about his manner, as though he's come on a matter of grave importance – that Social Services have found Carol's letters, perhaps, and told Royal Mail, even the police.

'Is everything okay?' says Albert. His nerves make him cough, the whole bed rattling with the strain.

'Shouldn't it be me asking you that question?'

'What do you mean?' he gasps.

'You're in hospital, Albert. They said you could have died.'

'Oh, that!' he replies, flush with relief. 'No, no, I'm fine. It was just a bug.'

There's a moment of silence, Darren still looking tense. 'Actually, I'm here on official business.'

Albert stiffens again as Darren reaches for something out of sight. When he turns back to face him, there's a large parcel in his hands, a mass of brightly coloured paper and curly pink bows, obviously too feminine for Darren's taste.

'One of the girls in the office did it,' he says, loud enough for everyone in the ward to hear.

'It's lovely.'

'And there's a card – everyone signed it. We probably should have done a get-well card too, but this one was already doing the rounds when we heard. Seemed a shame to waste paper.'

'No, it's lovely. And, anyway, who wants to be reminded of being sick?'

'Well, there are some get-well messages in there too.'

'Oh, of course, I mean it's the thought that counts, isn't it?'

He scans through the mass of scrawled greetings. Many of them are so hard to read, it will probably take him the rest of his life to figure out what they say. Only Mickey's message leaps from the page, the handwriting as lucid as the sentiment: 'Remember, you're almost dead. Make the most of what you've got left.'

'It's lovely,' says Albert. 'Thank you.'

'And, well, you know . . . it's never nice to hear someone's sick, especially when they're old, so we had a whip-round.' He hands an envelope to Albert. A few coins jangle at the bottom, but the rest is a thick wad of banknotes. Albert stares at them, open-mouthed.

'It's just a gift. I mean, in addition to all your statutory retirement benefits. The finance department will deal with those.'

'I'm speechless. I really am.'

Darren appears to relax, perhaps because he's touched by Albert's gratitude or maybe because he knows the end of the visit is now in sight. 'You still haven't opened your present.'

Albert blushes, unaccustomed to so much attention. He holds the package up, gives it a gentle squeeze. Beneath the shiny wrapping paper, it's soft to the touch.

As he peels the paper away, a cuff comes into view, and a collar. Even before a quarter of the paper is gone, Albert stops unwrapping and just stares at it.

A brand new Royal Mail coat.

'We figured the one you've got is probably getting a bit old. This should do you for another forty years.'

Albert's eyes begin to well, and even Darren is smiling now, looking so human and friendly, Albert regrets thinking him a wanker all these years.

'It's a shame you missed your own party,' says Darren, 'but we drank a toast to you.'

'So you still went ahead with it?'

'Well, you know, some of the lads had been looking

forward to it.' He hesitates, suddenly seems to regret mentioning it. 'You know how they like tea and cake.'

'I'm glad you all had a good time. Please tell everyone I said thank you. For this and everything. For a career I've been proud of.'

'It's been an honour, Albert.' He shakes his hand with surprising warmth. 'Remember to come and see us sometimes.'

Albert listens as he walks away, the sound of his footsteps so distinct he could only be a visitor – someone from the world outside, someone with things to do and impressions to make.

And not just any visitor, thinks Albert, as he begins to smile, but *my* visitor.

65

THIS IS NOT how it's supposed to be. For years, the prospect of a solo trip to Athens has been the light at the end of Carol's tunnel, the promise of an afterlife. In reality she's arrived at her hotel with red and puffy eyes, having cried for most of the flight and all the way into town.

Bob would doubtless have found the farewell note hours ago, positioned as it was beside some jam doughnuts in the kitchen. It wasn't a long letter, but she's fairly certain it would have distracted him from World of Warcraft for the rest of the day. By now the reality of the situation will be starting to bite: his first night alone, the first of many.

The thought of him crying only makes Carol cry more, not with regret at what she's done today, but at what she's done for the last eighteen years, spinning a web so tangled she doesn't know how either of them will ever break free.

It's never occurred to Carol that Greece gets cold in winter. Cooler, of course, but not cold. She's always imagined winter is when people stop dying of heatstroke and instead just wander the streets in shorts, looking jolly. In every picture she's ever seen of Greece, the landscape looks too parched and sun-baked for cold, wet days. And yet here she is in Athens and the weather feels no better than London, with the exception that in London she could just go home and read a book in her fluffy pyjamas. She could do that in Athens, too, but for the fact she hasn't brought her fluffy pyjamas – and even if she had, her hotel isn't the place to wear them. Dark and cold, it's better suited to an ascetic retreat, the kind of place to deny oneself food and water, or self-flagellate in atonement for some terrible sin. Even the bed feels specifically designed to punish; a place to lie awake at night and ponder where life went wrong.

It would be nice to say that Athens itself makes up for the experience, but it really doesn't. Carol is in no mood for sightseeing, but from what little she's seen it's Croydon with rubble, the perfect backdrop for days spent feeling bleak and tearful.

Desperate for comfort, she calls Helen.

'Carol, where are you?'

'Athens.'

'Bloody hell, Carol! Everyone's going mental with worry.'

'I'm fine,' she replies, already beginning to cry. 'How are Bob and Sophie?'

'Not great, but they'll survive. It's you I'm worried about.'

'I'm fine, really. I just need . . . Oh, God, I don't know . . .'

'You could have told me you were going to leave.'

'I didn't want you to stop me.'

'I'm a crap friend, I know that.'

'That's not what I mean.'

'But it's true. Look, there's something I didn't tell you last week and I've been feeling bad ever since.' The thought of Helen being deceitful is so shocking that Carol's tears begin to slow. 'It's about your dream.'

'God, Helen, is that all?'

'But I know what it means. I've always known. As soon as you told me, I knew. And I lied to you. I've been feeling so guilty, I even wrote you a letter last night and burned it in the garden.'

'Then it's no wonder I didn't get it.'

'Look, in your dream, your mother is you. It's your subconscious telling you that your old life is over. It's time to accept yourself for what you really are.'

'Accept myself for what? A total fuck-up?'

'Caro—'

'And a selfish bitch?'

'You're neither of those things.'

'That's not how I'm feeling right now.'

'That's because you're running away. Things don't miraculously fix themselves just because you spend four hours on easyJet.'

'I can't go back.'

'I'm not saying you should. You can come and stay with me for a while, for as long as you want.' Silence. 'And no lesbian *Fatal Attraction* stuff, I promise. Just get back here and we'll figure it out together, one day at a time.' Still no response. 'I'm just sorry I didn't say anything sooner.'

'It doesn't matter.'

'But it does. I've been so scared of losing you, it was like I wanted to lock you in a cage or something. Even though you've been miserable for so long, I was just thinking of myself . . .' Her voice cracks. 'I couldn't bear the thought of you going away . . .'

They fall silent; two women quietly becoming teary-eyed at three pounds per minute.

'Have I screwed everything up?' says Carol.

'Well, it's not the best thing you've ever done, I'll give you that. But it's not like you've killed anyone.'

'I just couldn't stay. Not any longer.'

'It's okay, Carol, it really is. I don't know how we're going to do it, but I know we'll sort this out.'

ALBERT HAS BEEN in hospital for less than a week, but from the safety of his bed the outside world has begun to seem like a dangerous, unpredictable place, so that even going home has become a daunting prospect.

'Don't worry, that's natural,' says Pat, as they prepare to leave. 'Once you're back, you'll wonder what all the fuss was about.'

If that's true, it doesn't apply to standing outside his building. As Pat gathers the last of his belongings from the car, he feels more intimidated than ever. The estate looms ominously all around him, a grey and threatening place of smashed glass and graffiti.

'Home, sweet home,' says Pat, without a hint of irony. 'I think you'll find there's someone upstairs who's been waiting to see you.'

'Gloria? She's here already?'

The prospect of seeing Gloria again makes even a piss-stained lift tolerable. And when the doors open on Albert's floor, Max is there too – an oddly reassuring reminder of life's continuity.

'That's my neighbour,' says Albert. He gives Max a cheery wave, but Max doesn't appear to recognize him. He just scurries indoors, a nervous animal running for cover. By the time they pass his flat, the place could be empty it's so still. Even the flowers speak of a quiet dereliction, their garish colours now silenced by neglect.

The emotion of Albert's reunion with Gloria would be more appropriate to two lovers separated by war, but he feels no shame. This cat is his life.

'We almost died together, didn't we? What an adventure.' He's still stroking her when he notices the wall above the window. 'The damp patch is gone!'

'Next time you need something done, you just let me know.'

'I don't know how to thank you,' he says, oblivious to the fact that a large patch of wall is now painted a totally different colour from the rest. 'You'll be getting a present this Christmas, I can tell you that much.'

'As long as you're not going to knit me a sweater. I have enough of those from my sister.' She bustles towards the front door. 'So it looks to me like you're all set, young man. I'll be back in touch in a day or two to see how you're getting on.'

'We can have some tea and cake.'

Pat's face lights up. 'I never say no to a slice of cake!' She pauses in the doorway and tries her best to look stern. 'Just remember it's cold out, so no more wandering the streets, do you hear me?'

67

CAROL GAVE HER telephone number to Helen – sensible Helen – on the agreement that Bob and Sophie need to know where she is, maybe even need to talk, and that she actually needs it too, regardless of whether it's going to be a pleasant experience. Which is why, when the phone starts to ring, she naturally assumes it's Bob.

She lets it ring for a while, intimidated by its harsh tone, a sound that doesn't augur well for the dialogue to come. Even as she picks it up, she doesn't know how to say what needs to be said.

'Bob?'

Deirdre's voice comes rushing down the line, poisonous in its anger.

'Carol? You should be ashamed of yourself!'

'Mother—'

'How could you do it, Carol? What were you thinking?'

Carol closes her eyes, unsure if she's trying to summon

a response or simply shutting down, her whole body beginning to liquefy in the onslaught.

'And the man's sick,' says Deirdre.

'He told you . . .'

'Somebody needed to. You obviously didn't consider it important. I can't believe you'd just abandon him—'

'Oh, for Christ's sake, Bob's a grown man! I know it was a stupid thing to do, but so was marrying him in the first place. I would expect my own mother to understand that.'

'Bob's been good to you. You were lucky to have him.'

'Don't you listen to anything I say? I don't love him. I've never loved him.'

'You married him.'

'Because I got pregnant! You don't have to love someone to fuck.'

'Please don't use that word.'

'He fucked me, I got pregnant, and in some moment of utter madness I thought I owed it to everyone to spend the rest of my life with him. I'm not sure at what point you decided to believe it was love, but that's always been your problem, hasn't it? Believing crazy things.'

'I know you don't approve of me.'

'At last the woman speaks some sense.'

'Well, maybe I'm disappointed with you too.'

'Yes, but the difference is you didn't feel a need to fuck half the men in Croydon just to get away from me.'

At the other end of the line, stunned silence. Then the tears begin, Deirdre's handkerchief inadvertently muffling the mouthpiece. 'Why are you always so mean to me?'

296

'And why can we never just speak honestly? I feel like I'm sifting through the crime scene of my life and your fingerprints are on everything.'

'Well, maybe I'm not happy either, had you ever thought of that? Maybe I never wanted any of this. You, your father. I knew I was making a mistake when I walked down the aisle, but you don't hear me whining about it.' As her words fade to silence, time itself seems to stop, even the streets of Athens reduced to a standstill. 'That's why I'm looking forward to the Second Coming,' she adds, her words sounding more and more like those of a lonely, lost child. 'Everything will be fine after that.'

For the first time, Carol wishes she was there at Deirdre's side, not for the joy of her company, but for the value of simply giving her a hug and telling her that this life – the only one she'll ever have – could be so much better if only she wants it to be. In the absence of Deirdre's ability to think as an adult, there's no point in dissecting the opium of her religious beliefs; no point in discussing the way her past has impacted on her present. Biology has given Deirdre the title of mother, but in every other respect Carol must be the parent, she can see that now. And if she can be the parent her own mother needs, then perhaps she can yet be the parent that Sophie needs too.

'Look,' says Carol, with a certainty and self-assurance she didn't know she possessed, 'I'm sorry your life has been unhappy, but I need you to work with me if we're going to save this relationship.'

'It's always nice to see you.'

'Well, thank you, but there's really more to it than that. Being close is something we have to do, not something we just miraculously are.'

'Yes, yes, of course.'

'For a start, I need you to be nicer to Dad, despite what he's done in the past. We're all going to move on, okay? We've all got to forgive each other and make a fresh start.'

'Yes . . .'

Her voice trails off into a silence that's begging for words Carol never thought she'd say – is frightened of saying – but the time has come to move beyond fear.

'I love you, do you know that?' She can hear Deirdre start to cry again. 'I haven't always wanted to, and to be honest you've never made it very easy, but I do. I don't know when I'm coming back, but when I do we can talk.'

'That'll be nice.'

'Yes,' says Carol, amazed at her own sincerity, 'yes, it will.'

68

PAT WAS RIGHT about coming home. It's night time now and Albert sits in front of the television – with the sound turned off, naturally – pondering how lucky he is. The biscuit tin is on his lap, the beginnings of a new friendship at his fingertips. Beside him, Gloria purrs happily in a fresh nest of tissue paper.

With everything in his life returning to normal, Carol is the obvious next step. It's true that Pat doesn't want him walking the streets, but surely it doesn't count if he knows where he's going? And, anyway, he has a nice new coat to keep him warm.

He wheezes gently and begins to cough. 'I think I'll go down there tomorrow. I might even take the whole tin with me. What do you think?' He glances at Gloria, his adviser on all things. 'Hmm, yes, maybe you're right. We don't want to overdo it, do we? One letter is plenty.'

69

CAROL HAS BROKEN it, she's sure of that now. She has taken her life and clumsily smashed it open, but in breaking it she's let in some light, and she's beginning to see what life might yet be.

They're still faint, these early rays of optimism – certainly not strong enough to soothe the sickening feeling that she's made a fool of herself while also hurting everyone she's ever cared about – but as she wakes up to a new day, she can at least believe there's a way through the wreckage.

Bob still hasn't called, his silence saying far more than a phone call ever could. He's probably spent the last two days comfort eating, so that by now the house is ankle-deep in empty Coke cans and plastic wrappers. It will only be a matter of days, even hours, before the rats come, and from there an outbreak of bubonic plague that will reduce Croydon to a ghost town, a festering mass grave within easy reach of the M25.

Despite her instincts, she picks up the phone and calls

him. She would just as soon pick up a rusty sword and disembowel herself, but she owes him this, she knows that.

It rings for some time before he answers, as though he can't decide whether he wants to talk, or perhaps can't find the phone in the chaos of the house.

'Hello?'

He sounds weak, frail, lost.

'Bob, it's me.'

Silence.

'I'm sorry, Bob.'

'And, what, you've only just figured that out?'

'I'm going to stay with Helen wh—'

'So it's really over, is it?'

'Yes, Bob. It's—'

He hangs up on her, their conversation – much like their marriage – brought to an abrupt conclusion.

Under the circumstances, she decides the call went relatively well. At the very least it established that he's still alive, and the anger in his voice is surely a good sign: proof of the fighting spirit he'll need to find his own path through the wreckage.

70

THE JOURNEY TO Carol's house is much pleasanter now that Albert knows where he's going. While he walks, he practises his lines one last time.

'Hello, Carol. My name's Albert. I got one of your letters, and I just wanted to say thank you.'

That seems nice and positive. He's even brought his favourite letter with him, just to prove his point. He doesn't need to tell her that he's read all the others too; that he knows about her wayward youth, for instance, or that her husband has lost a testicle. It will be enough to tell her she's inspired him and given him something to believe in. That's the right foundation for a solid friendship.

As he turns the final corner into her cul-de-sac, he finds himself catching his breath. During his time in hospital, he's imagined Carol and her neighbours all deciding they would rather live somewhere else – not only moving out, but also razing their houses to the ground just for good measure. Albert had half expected to find nothing but parched earth, no hope of ever discovering where Carol has gone.

But, no, everything looks just the same as before. The flag is still fluttering over the neighbourhood, albeit in a state of chronic disrepair; the gardens still look neat and well tended; and there's Carol's house, this time with a car in the driveway.

With a purposeful stride he's practised numerous times at home, Albert goes up to the house and rings the bell.

Moments later, Bob comes to the door, dishevelled, his eyes red and puffy.

He stands there, obviously waiting for Albert to say something.

'Is Carol in?'

Bob begins to cry.

'I'm sorry,' says Albert.

'No, it's just . . .' He glances at the coat. 'What is it you want?'

'Oh, I'm . . . I'm with Royal Mail. It's about some of Carol's letters.'

Bob shivers in the cold. 'You'd better come in for a moment.'

As Albert enters the house, it's clear that something is wrong. All the curtains are drawn shut, the floor covered with rubbish. Bob wanders through the living room, seemingly oblivious to the devastation around him.

'My wife's left me,' he says, as he collapses into an armchair and starts to cry again. 'I – I don't know what I'm going to do.'

Albert watches him for a moment. 'I once lost someone I loved,' he says gently. 'It was a long time ago, but I understand.'

It's hard to tell if Bob has heard him or not. He just sits there crumpled in the seat, his cheeks wet with tears.

In the long wait that follows, Albert realizes he's standing beside a shelf of family mementoes – so many trophies and prize certificates, it seems as though Sophie Cooper may one day take over the world. Among all the photos of a young girl winning things, there's only one of a woman the right age to be Carol. She doesn't look the way he'd imagined; not a Connie at all. Hers is the face of everyday life, the kind of woman he sees on the bus, at the supermarket, at the bank.

She stares out at him, her mop of unruly hair framing a look of vague desperation, as if the camera is recording a terrible mistake: her being in the wrong place with the wrong people.

Albert peers closer, engrossed now. Sure enough, her hands are on her lap, her fingers crossed.

'Tell me why you're here again?' says Bob, as he wipes his face with a sleeve.

'Your wife, er . . . she wrote some letters . . . a few weeks ago . . . but they were undeliverable.'

'So you're returning them or something?'

'Er, no.' He slips his hand into his pocket and pushes the letter further down. 'They were destroyed.'

'You what?' He sounds angry now.

'It's standard procedure.' He can hear the fear in his

voice. 'I just wanted to pop round and tell her how to stop it happening in the future.'

For a moment it looks like Bob is going to make a scene. Albert can imagine it spiralling out of control, going all the way to Darren, maybe even higher.

But, no, the pain is too strong. It pulls him back from the edge, draining the fight from his face. 'Well, it's too late now, isn't it? She's already said she'll never live here again.'

Albert tries to think of something encouraging to say, but nothing comes to mind.

'Well, I ought to be leaving,' he says quietly.

He waits for a response, but Bob sits motionless, stares at the floor.

As Albert turns for the door, he glances one last time at Carol's picture and gives her a fond smile, glad that they've met at last.

71

It's easier to forgive Athens its shortcomings now that Carol is beginning to forgive her own.

There's one hill that seems to tower over the city and, on the spur of the moment, Carol decides she will climb it. It feels inappropriate to think of this as sightseeing: everything is still too raw for that. This is exercise, maybe even therapy – after all, aren't troubled people supposed to get out and do this sort of thing?

Before long, she's climbing streets that are deceptively steep and the distant hilltop appears more derisive. If she can't even make it this far, she'll certainly never make it to the summit. By the time she sees signs for a funicular railway, her commitment to hiking is long gone. Convinced that she's the victim of Greek air pollution rather than years of a poor diet and inadequate exercise, it isn't a difficult decision to take the train. As it gently pulls her up a gradient that surely would have killed her had she tried it on foot, she consoles herself that she's already done enough exercise to flood her body with endorphins; there's no point being greedy.

Carol is still waiting for the train to leave the tunnel when it arrives at the top and the other passengers begin to get off. As she steps out from the station, however, it feels appropriate to have been transported here in the womb-like confines of a concrete tube: her passage through the heart of the mountain was less a train ride than a process of personal transformation, a journey that has both literally and figuratively transported her to a higher place. From this vantage-point, Athens fans out in every direction, an intriguing sprawl to distant hills and sea. The city hasn't been quite as she imagined, but after the last few days – not to mention the last eighteen years – a discovery like this seems par for the course. Even amid its scars and disappointments, Athens has a certain magic, she can see that now – and in the middle of it all, the Parthenon rising up on its rocky pedestal.

She tries to keep reminding herself not to feel too happy. She is, after all, a terrible woman who's done terrible things, both as a wife and a mother. Yet then she looks out at the view and her spirits lift regardless.

It's even more ethereal as she zigzags down the hill's steep, forested flanks, the air occasionally punctured by the scent of wild sage and thyme, aromas that she's previously only known in bottles and plastic packaging.

It's hard to reconcile this with her days stalking the herb aisle in a Croydon supermarket. As implausible as it seems, she is on her way to becoming the kind of person she'd always hoped to meet; not a woman who cooks with herbs but who actually walks among them, emancipated and free. It strikes her as perverse that this is the true nature of life, that a seemingly simple act – leaving an unhappy marriage, for instance – can take decades, whereas something as hopelessly complex as personal transformation can take just a matter of days.

It's the kind of thing she wants to sing aloud, to stop passers-by and share with them – a tale of reinvention, the discovery of a hope she once thought extinct. More than anything, she wishes her father could see her now, to witness what kind of woman she's becoming. She can imagine the contortion of his lips, what passes for a smile in the immobility of his world – proof that somewhere deep inside he's punching the air and shouting from the rooftops that his daughter has come of age, that the girl who lost herself so many years ago has found herself at last.

Even after the forest has given way to city streets choked with traffic, Carol walks with a spring in her step, surprisingly at ease with the chaos now. This is her city, not despite its imperfections but precisely because of them. Mistakes have been made, things that should be beautiful are not, and yet life roars on. For someone like Carol, there is solace in these streets.

As she turns a corner and the Parthenon comes back into view, her smile says it all. Life has turned on its axis and all things are possible once more.

72

SHE WAS CONFUSED when it arrived. It's true her name was on the envelope, and the letter began with the words 'Dear Sophie', every line executed in meticulous pen strokes, but still she had no idea who he was.

She wanted to ask her father if he'd ever heard of Albert, but the weeks that followed Carol's departure were not the best time to engage Bob in conversation. So instead she found herself reading the letter again and again, trying to pinpoint Albert's exact position in the family nebula.

He certainly seemed familiar with certain aspects of her parents' marriage, and he was a subtle advocate for Carol at a time when her proponents were few and far between. But most of all it was his *concern* that confused Sophie. This man she'd never met, had never even heard of, asking her if she was all right. And the thing was, she didn't feel all right, hadn't felt all right for years, in fact, and somehow it was easier to explain that to a total stranger. So she replied.

*

Today of all days, she thinks of Albert. How their corre-
spondence began. How the years slowly eroded the distance
and formality between them, a young girl who needed a
kindly grandfather as much as he needed a family of his own.

She thinks of this as she stands at a graveside with her
husband and two young sons, watching as her real grandfather is laid to rest. Although she tries to feel some grief as
the coffin sinks out of view, all she can summon is relief for
his sake. A windswept cemetery within earshot of Gatwick
is hardly the ideal resting place, but he did not have an ideal
existence. If nothing else, it is some consolation that a man
who suffered Deirdre in life would likely have no problem
with the constant roar of jet engines in death.

And then the rain starts, slowly at first, barely noticeable,
but as another plane screams overhead, the wind picks
up and soon the rain is blowing sideways. For a moment,
Deirdre just stands there, looks frail and bewildered, as
though she can no longer tell the difference between the
weather and her own emotions. Sophie and Carol shepherd
her to one of the waiting cars, the small group of mourners
quickly scattering behind them.

By the time everyone regroups at Deirdre's house, there's a
damp sense of camaraderie; a general belief that the worst is
now behind them in every sense, and perhaps the day might
yet be salvaged by a stiff drink and some warm food.

Bob is here to pay his respects, though it's a little odd to
see him without his wife. Under normal circumstances she's
more like an appendage than a spouse. Perhaps it was the

thought of seeing Carol that kept her away, or maybe she just has more common sense than everyone gives her credit for. There is, after all, no good reason to attend the cold, wet funeral of a total stranger.

In her absence, Bob and Carol chat longer than they have in many years. Sophie watches their body language, can still remember the bitterness that used to colour their every exchange, but all she can see now are two proud grandparents who know each other intimately, for better and for worse.

Bob's expanding waistline makes him seem shorter and rounder these days, his grey hair giving him the jolly appearance of a suburban Father Christmas. Compared to him, Carol is an ageless pixie, a woman who looks healthier and more vibrant in her fifties than she ever did when she was young.

Carol's husband – a sculptor of increasing renown – is with Deirdre on the far side of the room. They sit in a reverent silence, the expression on Deirdre's face suggesting she's just realized what her own funeral will look like.

Helen is here with her second husband, a man in his sixties more commonly seen in shorts and hiking boots. It's become a family joke that, thanks to his passion for the great outdoors, Helen's natural habitat is now a muddy field; that her idea of a dinner party is cold baked beans eaten off a plastic plate. As hard as it is to fathom, even Jane and her kids sometimes join them on their camping trips, her pubescent aggression long since replaced by a nondescript and forgettable personality. And yet Helen seems thrilled with the transformation – not because Jane has achieved anything remarkable, but rather because she's faded into anonymity, something that would have seemed impossible back when she was a teenager.

These are the things Sophie looks forward to sharing with Albert when she next sees him; updating him about all these people, many of whom he's met. She still smiles at the memory of finally introducing him to Carol. The way she'd said, 'Mum, this is Albert. You sort of know each other already . . .'

In his mid-eighties now, he occasionally reminds Sophie that his days are drawing to an end. And when she tells him not to say things like that, he just gives her his gentle smile – the same smile that has accompanied all his lessons about acceptance and forgiveness. He says it's been a wonderful life, but he must go eventually because he has a date to keep. A date with a beautiful woman he's not seen in a long, long time.

Acknowledgements

MY FRIENDS AND family do a great job of putting up with my absences, whether physical or mental. I thank all of them for their patience. With memories of Shanghai, I would especially like to thank Dexter, Datsun, Peter, Kat, Steve, Sam and Mike. In Hong Kong, thank you to Reinhold and David for years of friendship, and to Sarah Allen for being a mad and extraordinary human being. In Berlin, my thanks go to Kim-Patrick, Juka, Lars, Betti, Michi, Hiro, Hannes, Nico, Denny, Karl, Henning, Robert and Ewa. Thank you also to Javier and Greta in Barcelona.

One of the joys of writing a book is the collaborative process that follows long months of solitary confinement. I am very grateful to Tricia Davey, who found me even before I found myself. Heartfelt thanks likewise go to the team at Peters Fraser & Dunlop, especially Robert Caskie, Alexandra Cliff and the wonderful Rachel Mills. I am also immensely thankful to everyone at Constable & Robinson for welcoming me with such enthusiasm, in particular Victoria

Hughes-Williams and Emily Burns. Most of all I thank my exceptional agent, Juliet Mushens, who is everything the perfect agent should be and so much more.